CASHMERE DREAMS

CASHMERE DREAMS

Sam Braden, IV

ISBN: 978-1-971712-08-6

Quill and Company Publishing

QuillandCompany.com
TheQuillandCompany@gmail.com

Dedication

For my son, Sam Braden V—You are the reason I chose growth over comfort, healing over hiding, and purpose over mere survival. Everything I am becoming is for you. For those who came before me—whose prayers, pain, and perseverance paved a way I didn't always understand, but walked in every day. And for anyone still fighting to find their way out—this is for you.

Contents

RECORD I - THE SURVIVAL YEARS:

The raw, gritty origin story...

SIDE A - Out the Mud: Origin & Survival

Birth, environment, and early years.

Track 1: Kush & Corinthians

"Before my name was on a ballot, I saw a blade. Before I ever held a mic, I had to hold my peace like I was never afraid. Screams in dark alleys behind apartments, praying in the midst of kush clouds in the wind. Gotta have heart, only the strong survive in the end."

Deep in the soul of the Dirty South, the air tasted of fresh thick molasses, chopped wood, and suffocating clouds of sulfurous gas. Back when Mama told me that the Bible was supposed to save you; life, without a doubt, had its own gospel.

Yet it didn't come in red letters.

It came from loud sirens, screams, and deeply rooted pain. In addition to missed meals and broken-hearted mothers, who appeared as though they aged a decade each time rent was due. The dormant parts of their heart were engraved with unspoken stress, like a maze that no sermon could sort out.

Mama always was humming hymns while folding the clothes, after bringing them from the laundromat down the road. Her voice didn't usually go above a whisper. But you could hear the spirit of the words over the propped fan in the window. And she would fan herself like we were sitting in the church.

I understand though. Smh. Since it was always hot, even in the shade. Her voice had an old-school soulful, cool vibe, like a breeze pushing through the heavy dampness and stickiness of the city.

Each night she would read the same scripture out loud, talkin' about love. Mama always told me that nothing is greater than love. So it was obvious that Corinthians was her favorite book in the Bible.

"Love is patient, love is kind…"

Back then, those words hit different, almost recharging the core of my spirit. I thought if I spoke them enough, the lights would not get cut off, again. Then the fridge wouldn't be empty.

And just maybe, just maybe, Daddy would come back. I always hoped that he would stay longer, more than just a weekend.

The world outside our door, though, moved to a totally different beat. Slower, but also so much heavier too. Kinda like bass shaking in a Box Chevy with the windows down; smoke lingering out comparable to evading spirits. With exhaust fumes that smelled like burnt desperation.

At that time, I was in a fight that I wasn't aware of and didn't have a chance to win.

I was only twelve years old.

And we had to move again. Our third apartment in only two years. This one is smaller and in the worst part of the neighborhood. Brown water coming from the taps and it seemed like roaches popped up every ten minutes.

We didn't even escape the first month without an eviction notice being taped to the door.

I will never forget how Mama was staring at it; it seemed like it was almost a full hour. But, she didn't make a sound or say anything at all. Just gazing into the unknown, and her eyes were beyond heavy, flooded with entire oceans of tears.

You could hear the silent, absolute hopelessness of a broken woman. *And man, I hated to see it. But what could I do?*

Nothing. But dream of an easier, better life.

During the same week, I felt it, almost like it was buried in my chest.

Bass.

But not like music class. Different. Deep. Real.

Kind of knockin' rumblin' outta trunks that makes your ribs shake. For the first time I heard somebody ride down our block bumping music. Beating down the block, trunk rattling the speakers; vibrating the essence of the car. It was a sermon with 808s.

And I remember saying to myself: *This what* **freedom** **sound like. Loud, authentic, and proud.**

Every single day, I remember feenin' for that feeling. It was a knowing. An understanding beyond words.

Especially when I had to cut through that back alley behind our building one evening. On this day, the sky seemed to be bruised and overwhelmed from the heat. And the sun was hidden underneath the fire escapes, resulting in a dark sky the same color as old, dehydrated blood.

A day like this most people would snap for any reason.

And this type of alley was unusually quiet. Unnerving. Spine-chilling.

There was a lingering aura that had you looking over your shoulder. A strange kind of silence making your skin crawl.

While I was trying to step carefully, my shoes were crunching the gravel.

Then I heard it: a car door slammed.

Loud. Earsplitting. Sudden. **BOOM.**

Ringing like a gunshot.

A man stepped out. Fragile, weak, shoulders tense. His entire being pulsating.

Gripping a small ziplock bag close to his chest. White powder inside like crushed snow that didn't have no business in this heat.

Then another man just popped up. Felt like…out of nowhere.

Damn. Seemed like he was twenty feet tall. Wide body-frame, menacing dark eyes that have seen too much and cared about almost nothing. His skin was oily with sweat, reflecting off the streetlights in a jet-black, glossy finish.

He didn't walk like normal, he covered the entire space.

Instantly, I was stuck. Couldn't move.

"Where IS....my money?" the tall man roared.

The other man mumbled vaguely as he trembled uncontrollably, struggling to keep his balance. While a few crumbled dollar bills were slithering halfway out of his pocket.

"Uh, uh......I, I think—I might got.... got....most of it," he slurred.

Wrong answer.

The tall man hit him with enough power to shake the ground beneath him. A backhand that cracked across the smaller man's face, bounced back off the concrete like a beat drop. The sound echoed for a moment with a haunting vibration.

He dropped, as his knees scuffed the ground. The bag burst open, as the white powder consumed the air and descended into the pavement like sugar drizzling in a nightmare.

Then, I saw it. Long, sharp, chrome blade. Gleaming in the yellowish-brown glow of the lone streetlight.

The tall man leaned in close. Pressed the knife against the man's throat with the intimacy of a secret.

"Next time, no talkin'. I'm just gon' leave you leakin'."

Yeah, after that I don't remember. Anything.

My body acted instinctively, without thought. I shot outta that alley quick, lungs burning like crazy.

I ran until my mouth was dry, not from fatigue, but from sheer terror.

Vision was blurred and the sound of my heartbeat drowned everything else. My hands were trembling so bad by the time I got back to the apartment.

Looking down I gripped the chain that Mama gave me. It was a little gold cross. I pressed it into my hands creating a calm, affirmed that I still existed.

But.... now something was different.

Faith and bullets were supposed to be opposites.

Except that night, they felt like cousins. Two different kinds of shields in a war zone.

Sleep remained elusive that night, I lay wide eyed on my bed looking. I stared at the ceiling, charting the pattern of cracks as though they offered solutions. The world outside our apartment felt sharper now, like I was seeing it without the blur of childhood.

That moment in the alley had changed everything.

No one was safe. I had to do something.

The next morning, Mama made white rice and eggs like she always did when she was trying to keep things normal. She hummed her usual gospel tune— "His Eye Is on the Sparrow"—and I just listened.

This time….it hit a little different…. because my entire world had shifted underneath me. The rice tasted like rubber; the hymn felt like a delicate, desperate lie.

Then, Mama started reading Corinthians, in a peaceful, soft voice…. slightly above a whisper.

"Love is patient, love is kind. It does not envy, it does not boast..."

Yet, the only thing I could see was blood. All I could hear was that man begging and smell the fear that filled the air in that alley.

"Eat, baby," she said, tapping my hand. "You need strength to face the day."

Strength, is a strange word isn't it? It felt very different now, like a new thing.

Kind of like metal. A cold, hard reality you had to create for yourself.

At school, I watched people differently now. I could see the armor they all wore, almost like a protective barrier.

Boys laughed too loud, kept a hand on their strap, and one eye on the door. Girls moved with grace but carried razorblades under their tongues.

Jokes cut souls like weapons. Smirks protected hearts like shields.

And Kush was the religion.

They passed it under bleachers and outside, behind gym doors. Js that were rolled tight, sweet-smelling aura, aroma therapy. It was a temporary baptism in smoke, washing away the shame and the hunger.

Some people believed it helped calm their demons. And made the trouble of the world slow down just enough to feel endurable.

And even though...I hadn't smoked yet. I understood why they did.

Was it noise? Fear? Or rage?

No.It came from knowing the world had no place for you.

So, you had to take it by force. That stuff simply needed numbing, no easy solution.

That night, I sat on the porch while Mama folded laundry inside. The sky was smeared with purple and orange. Summer air hung heavy like wet cotton.

A group of boys walked by, wearing black hoodies, and ski masks. This would be normal if it wasn't 85 degrees outside. Their eyes, visible through the holes, were vacant and old, like they were already ghosts.

So, some people mumbled, laughed, and made jokes sharp enough to stab. Then, one of the dudes in the hoodies looked at me, and nodded—half challenge, half invitation.

But I didn't nod back.

I wasn't ready to be one of them. Not yet.

But, I also knew that I wasn't the same innocent boy I was before that night in the alley either.

The next few days blurred. I took the long way home.

Hoodie up. Eyes sharp. Avoiding the alley like it was a cursed place.

Yet and still, it pulled at me regardless. Like a scar you couldn't stop touching.

So, I went back.

Same place. Same silence. But the blood was gone. And so was the bag.

Just cracked concrete and a few random joint roaches. The only residue of the violence was the phantom smell of fear.

Still, I could feel it.

Pain leaves its residue on the soul. So the alley was smeared with something permanent.

I bent down. Touched the spot where the man had bled. It was warm, almost like the concrete still remembered.

"Yo," a menacing voice said behind me.

Shit.

I damn near jumped out of my skin.

Then, a man leaned against the alley wall, smokin' a black. Hoodie. Dark jeans. Mouth full of gold teeth.

His eyes were flat, sharp like a snake.

"What up? What chu' need?"

I swallowed. "I'm good. Just… walkin'."

He smirked. "Ain't nobody just walkin' through **here**."

He moved in close enough for me to smell the liquor and weed on his breath. Not too aggressive, but very present.

He smelled exactly like the life I didn't want, but knew was inevitable.

"You saw **somethin'**….**Didn't you**?"

I stood still, no response, just staring at him.

"You ain't tell nobody?"

"Hell naw. I ain't said shit."

"Smart." He took another puff. Then, blew it out slow.

"You **SHOULD** keep your mouth shut…..you'll live longer."

Then he was gone.

When I got home, Mama was asleep in her chair. Bible open on her lap like a guard dog. I sat on the floor next to her, leaned my head against her leg.

"You okay, baby?" she said softly, with her eyes closed.

"Yeah"…….Even though I knew that I never would be.

I was beyond shook. Because I saw something that I couldn't unsee it. Couldn't unfeel it. It had clawed its way into the quiet space behind my ribs.

Couldn't unlearn what I been through:

Felt like this crazy world took a huge bite outta me.

So, all I could do was hold Mama's chain real close to me.

Not because I thought that it would save me.

But it reminded me of the "good 'ol days", before that day in the alley. When life was so different and seemed easier.

Maybe Corinthians wasn't wrong.

Love is patient.

And kind……

But it wasn't nothing like that **'round here**. Not here.

Because 'round here?

Love was ice cold.

And it existed without a soul.

Like an unfamiliar guest from another dimension.

And maybe—just maybe…..this beautiful struggle—was merely a **contradiction for love.**

A savage, ugly kind of love you earned by surviving it.

Track 2: The Blueprint

"Dropping bars on this microphone….I let the ink spill from my pen into old, dirty notebooks. Carving out my escape, makin' it hard to breathe, the weak ones always shook.
Before I ever dropped a mixtape, I put the truth on every street corner, and every block. My life is too real, the wrong move can make ya heart stop…"

Man…the sun was barely up, but them streets never slept. The block bled secrets from the concrete, murmuring soulful melodies of intense pain.

Like a low-frequency buzz of broken hearts beating out of sync.

The pulse of the city was vibrating through my entire body, walking through the neighborhood early that morning.

I didn't sleep much the night before, my eyes were bloodshot.

Yet, I still couldn't put my pen down, especially not since that first cypher with Tru Skyye. There was something infectious about how she looked at me and challenged me……it lit a fire that I never felt before.

The atmosphere was consumed with weed smoke and fried chicken. Kind of felt like I was walking through a backyard cookout.

But in my city it was a melting pot of poverty, hunger, and visions untold, while the world was falling apart.

When I hit the corner, I was looking for a pen in my pocket. But I knew I didn't need no pad or pencil to feel my lyrics. And feeling those 808s slappin' in my spirit, made my heartbeat faster.

Now, my mind was racing, trying to stay two steps ahead. Plotting, scheming on the next move like a game of chess. Except the board was broken concrete, with faded graffiti, coated with residue of broken glass from cheap liquor bottles.

Then, I saw my girl….. Tru Skyye posted up against the streetlight, with a cloud of smoke coming from her J like a ghost hugging the air.

She was built different…. Tru was never outta her element, she was the block.

Her long braids swung with every movement…..and those…..

Pretty. Brown. Eyes.

And her body….it was crazy. Words couldn't even describe……

MAN…..SMH.

But….her *eyes*…..

They always had that spark to them, like she knew something you didn't.

Even though she usually didn't say too much…..but when she did, her words were heavy. Never light.

Like a perfectly weighted stone breaking glass.

"You still haven't put the pen down, huh?"

She said to me. I just grinned, shaking my head, trying not to smile.

"What can I say? It's too many stories that need to be told."

Tru hit the J again, blowing the smoke in the air. "Some of them stories need to be forgotten. So new ones can be written."

I just looked at her. But I felt *every word* she said.

"You always think so big? Everything can't be fixed by spittin' a few bars."

She pushed off from the lamppost, stepping into his personal space with a slow, deliberate movement. *The intimacy of her closeness was both electric, and a challenge.*

"Nah. It ain't about fixin' nothing. It's showing people what's been there the whole time. You don't fix the broken. You just make it loud enough for people to hear it."

I let that sit in my chest. She was right.

My music wasn't gonna *"fix"* the world. It was about making people see it. The ugliness, beauty, and struggle. I wasn't trying to be some hero. I was just trying to speak my truth.

"Have you ever thought about the bigger picture?" Tru's voice became softer, but even heavier.

"This... mixtape thing, the rhymes, the covers—you think that's gonna get you out of here? Out of this cycle?"

SMH. I started looking down at the ground. Wasn't used to people getting that deep with me. Tru wasn't just talking about the streets. She was talking about something deeper, something that hit closer to home.

This was about the hereditary defeat, and generational gravity that held our community down.

"You got an exit plan?" I shot back, the words slipping out before I could stop them. But I didn't expect it to sound so... bitter.

Tru's eyes never left my sight. There was no anger in her expression—just understanding.

"You think I'm here because I don't know *how this place works*?"

She glanced over her shoulder, the crack of a smirk touching her lips.

"I been through it. I've seen what it can do to you if you let it. I'm gonna get out and drag as many of us with me as I can. This place doesn't define me, Cash."

I wanted to say something slick back to her. But I couldn't because she was right.

She peeled back a layer I wasn't ready to show anyone.

"Man... that's heavy," I muttered, scratching the back of his head. Then, pulled out a crumpled piece of paper from my jacket, and slid it toward her. It was a sketch of my next mixtape cover.

The paper was stained with the ink of both my frustration, and ambition. The cover was a mixture of disjointed images: loose chains, a bloody microphone, and in the skyline of my city, swimming in a pool of broken promises.

Tru eyed it for a moment, her fingers tracing the edges. "I like it," she said softly. "It's raw. But it's missing something. It's too clean."

My eyebrows raised. "Too clean?"

She gave me the paper.

"Yeah. You're trying too hard to make it pretty. Art don't need to be pretty, Cash. It needs to be real.

Make people feel like they got punched in the chest. You wanna really make a statement? Then make 'em uncomfortable. Let the streets breathe through that cover."

Thinking. I stared at the cover, trying to see it from her perspective. And then, like a switch flipping inside my brain, I got it!

This wasn't about perfection. It wasn't even about seeking approval from people. It was about making them feel the weight of everything left unsaid, everything buried in the concrete jungle.

"Uncomfortable, huh?" I muttered. And I felt a fire ignite inside of me that had never been there.

Tru nodded, tossing her J to the ground and grinding it under her boot. "Art is war. You don't go to war trying to play nice."

The way she said it was from a place of seeing too many people give up. And they never knew how to fight.

The look in her eyes said she knew what was inside of me, even if I didn't.

So, I took the paper back, balled it up and tossed it in the air. And it floated like a promise to the ground.

"Guess we're gonna see if I can make 'em bleed then."

Tru didn't smile. She didn't need to. We both knew that this was only the beginning.

Later that night, I was alone in my room, with a dim glow of a single light bulb hanging overhead. It smelled like weed roaches and day-old pizza. The radio was on low in the background, static crackling between the stations. Yet my mind was far from the music.

While my notebook was open, the echo of Tru's words reverberated through my head repeatedly.

Seemed like for hours, I sat and just created without overthinking. Then, it all began to take shape: *The Blueprint*.

It was a collage of colors merging, symbols linking, and a visual scream of everything unspoken.

This was the personification of decay, hopelessness, and rare sparks of brutal beauty in my reality. Imperfect lines. Unpolished edges. And simply raw emotion, like the world outside.

Looking at the cover, I couldn't help but smile. As my heart raced, I knew it. This was my time, and I could feel it.

My only *ticket* outta here.

This was more than music. It was time to make **history**.

That next day, I dropped my first official mixtape. The streets were rockin' with it hard for weeks. It was undeniable. Not just the theme, tracks, or cover. It was the reality check, showing us that we have been "playing the wrong game". And the rest of the world was using us as pawns, while hiding the plan in plain sight.

For the first time, I felt the love and heartbeat of the city. This was more than a mixtape; it was the start of a revolution. And with me and Tru? It was just the beginning.

Track 3: Pimp Hard

"Cashmere got the game on fire, seducing the streets and women, but it ain't no love. Big J's words colder than steel, hittin' hard like a glove.
But Tru's warnings fade into the background, drowned out by the noise of survival. Still in the end, he knows loyalty is the only way to the city's revival."

The world I saw existed through two sets of lenses: rose-colored in my dreams, and bloodshot when I was awake.

This game could easily distort a man's vision. There were days full of gold chains, stacks of money, and women melting at the thought of my name.

But the rest was filled with trap houses and empty promises. Not to mention, the haters preying on my downfall, all of them lost in a maze of delusion.

And that summer, the streets got way too hot. Air was thick with humidity and tension; feeling like it was the calm before the storm. *The type of heat that made the street sweat out its sins.*

At this point, I wasn't a young boy still sketching out my dreams in a notebook. Now, I was a grown man building a legacy and reclaiming what was taken before I was born.

I was charismatic, and a smooth talker, but they knew you couldn't just play with me.

My ways were strategic. I studied the art of seduction. Even the art of war.

This was about more than just getting women. But don't get it twisted; I could have them wrapped around my finger at any moment. This was about a bigger *game*.

I walked it like I talked it. That made it easy to convince anyone that I was the man.

My presence was magnetic, a smooth mix of charm and menace. No woman could manipulate me into anything that wasn't real. And no hustler could scam me on any transaction.

I had game for sale, dreams for profit. But the funny part was, I started believing my own words.

But the game?

The game never cared about anyone or anything. There was no loyalty. There was no love. Just players, who understood that there was a tragic end that was inevitable.

That's why even though I was on a current high, I understood what was coming. It's like dancing on the edge of a cliff, embracing the fall.

On this night, the walls of the trap house were a faded dirty off-white. The energy was filled with a stale aroma of burnt crack smoke. And old school music blasting through a broken radio.

But there I was, at the kitchen table, with my hands grippin' the cold steel of my strap. My eyes focused on the grind, table filled with bags of green, pills, and powder.

Tru was right there with me; you could see her silhouette in the doorway. I respected her because she moved fearlessly.

But tonight, there was a look of concern, like it was something coming she didn't wanna see.

A look that I couldn't totally understand. Though, eventually I would. It's wild to me, that she could still see the little boy inside of me.

"Dave, are you sure you wanna do this?" Tru said, her words floated through the room.

Initially, I was quiet. Then, I began scanning the space around me, the walls covered with random graffiti, waiting for the drop to happen. The plan was to see the money, then give him the bag, and we leave.

"Yeah," I said, slow trying to convince myself. "Ain't no time to turn back now." My words were solid, but they lacked the conviction of my lyrics.

"You keep running with these dogs, Cash, they gonna chew you up. Ain't no loyalty in this shit. It's all a lie. You're feeding into it, and you don't even see it."

When I looked at her, I knew that she was keepin' it real. Just like always, but I was in too deep now.

This time though, it was more powerful than any so-called "truth" I ever heard on the streets. Honestly, this was the very truth that I didn't want to acknowledge. Tru always said things to me in a different way. She never said anything that was random or casual. Her words had a rhythm to them, a beat that resonated with my soul.

The deal went down almost exactly as planned.

Money exchanged hands; the bags transferred. And I could feel the cold chrome against my ribs, reminding me of the price.

But then, there was a loud thunderous knock at the door.

It was a sharp sound, ricochetting through the whole trap like a warning.

Tru's eyes became rigid, focused on the door.

My heartbeat sped up so fast and loud that I couldn't even hear the music. That knock was familiar. But with a much different tone.

The door swung open, and it was him.

Big J.

His massive frame filled the doorway like a wall, blocking out the dim light from the hallway. See, Big J had a reputation in the neighborhood: money, power, and demanding respect. He owned the block. And tonight, I was caught up in the middle.

"You thought you could steal from me and walk away, Cashmere?"

Big J's voice rumbled like thunder, vibrating in the entire trap house. And it shook any remaining ounce of confidence I might've had.

Everything stood still, even our shadows. Big J's eyes were beyond cold, and you could tell he didn't care about a young hustler like me.

I didn't budge.

"Ain't nobody stealing from you. I'm just playing the game. You don't own it, J."

My words slipped out sharper than I intended, but I didn't care. I wasn't scared anymore. I was Cashmere. In this moment, I knew I could take on the whole damn world.

Now my chest was out, displaying false courage and heart.

Big J didn't blink. His look was numb.

"The game? You think you're playing the game, huh? You ain't nothin'. You don't make no rules. You're just another fool walking the same path they all walked before you. And it ain't no talkin' outta this? Nah. The game gonna chew you up and leave you in the gutter."

At this point, my stomach had moved into my throat. And I wanted to pull the strap, and pop that man, to show him what time it was.

Still, I knew, when you draw your piece in this world, you become another number in the game. Then, you join the rest of the forgotten souls in the streets.

Tru stepped toward him, her eyes wide open.

"You don't own him, J. Or this block, either. You might think you're the king, but you don't own nothin'."

She stepped into the path of the bullet meant for me, sacrificing her silence for my life.

Big J's smile faded, his eyes narrowing as he took a step forward, closing the gap between them.

"You better watch your mouth, girl. Do you know me?!"

But Tru didn't back down. She never did.

My hand jerked by my side, though I knew pulling the strap was the wrong move.

Especially, not when everything I was running from was closing in on me. And with the intense gravity of Big J's presence.

Big J's gaze shifted from Tru back to me.

"You can't play this game? Boy, it'll eat you alive. You better pay attention and learn what it's really about. The game ain't never love you. And sure as hell don't respect you."

Beyond nervous, my heart was racing and hands were sweating, but I stood ten toes down. I wasn't gonna let anybody play with me.

Big J wasn't tellin' me something new. The problem was, I wasn't sure if it mattered to him.

Big J took a step back, with a cold stare sizing me up.

"Enjoy the game, Cashmere. 'Cause one day, it'll turn its back on you. When it does, no one will save you."

As the door slammed, I could feel an anxiety beyond paranoia that I had never experienced. But I was glad that Tru stood by my side, as we remained in silence.

No words from either of us.

Though I knew Tru was disappointed, and it was more deafening than any threat from Big J.

Now, the game of the streets had me.

Even though I was playing a different game, I still needed to survive. But at some point, the game would turn on me, just like it did everyone else.

Track 4: Sermons & Mixtapes

"Cashmere walks the line between pulpits and pistols, spiritual soliloquies echoing over gun shells. Mixtapes drippin' like candle wax- filled soulful, beats with bass cause pain sells.
Brothers grippin' glocks, caught in a war zone, lost souls on the cracked pavement. So we hit the booth, spittin' truth thru these 808s, until we make it."

See, I had always lived in the space between contradictions. Raised in the Bible Belt, the echoes of mama's prayers and the "end of days" sermons from church had always hit deep in my soul. Every single word stuck to my lungs, fighting with the kush smoke I inhaled.

"Thou shalt not kill," the preacher would always say, voice booming like thunder as the congregation responded in praise and worship.

There was a different story when the streets spoke. Violence was the currency, and the only option was to survive. The street sermon was: *Get money or be silenced.*

In trap houses, no saints or sinners, just players, hustlers, and bodies dropping when the game ended.

Sunday mornings were always hard.

When I came to St. Luke's, I usually smelled like weed and bourbon from the night before. And it was the cheap bourbon, creating a permanent dark stain on the clean linen of my spirit. So, I constantly felt like a hypocrite.

Mama's Bible was the glue that kept me going. You could tell that she had been using it daily because it was worn-down to pieces. And it was usually on the coffee table at home. Every morning, Mama asked for me to pray with her before she went to work.

Most of the time I did, but it was a struggle. *I always wondered what made her faith so strong?*

She had the faith of a steady lighthouse, a symbol of hope that conflicted with our environment. The code of the streets didn't line up with our spiritual beliefs. So, I was at a fork in the road. What should I follow?

It was either: Church or the streets. To me, I felt like I was floating in a sea of contradictions between two worlds. And these two worlds were dragging me in opposite directions.

Church promised redemption, and forgiveness, in the sermons that I heard preached. But when the trap house door closed, the idea of salvation appeared to be a luxury.

Thou shalt not kill, but what if you're already dead inside?

What if the only way to feel alive is to balance the church and streets?

Did every choice we made already have our names carved into a list of inevitable sins? Was the street your cross to bear, and survival was your scripture?

And what if the ultimate sin was being a coward?

The first time I picked up a mic, it was in a dimly lit basement studio, surrounded by smoke and distorted beats. I poured my soul into that first mixtape.

The tracks were hard, raw, and full of swag about how I hustled my way to the top. But with every verse, the weight of the streets began to catch up with me. The mic was supposed to be my way out, but it became a magnet for the darkness that I was running from.

I stopped rapping about money and women, about power and control. The beats slowed down, the swagger faded, and I found myself confessing truths I didn't want to hear.

My raps were about angels with pistols, saints with gold grills, and holy warriors who bled just like I did. Finally, it hit me that my music was a desperate, loud prayer.

But it wasn't until Tru showed up that the full weight of contradictions hit me like a freight train. She always knew how to read me better than I knew myself.

I saw too many of the streets' lies for too long, and every time she looked at me, it was like she saw through the bravado to the broken man underneath.

We were sitting on the roof one night, the distant hum of the city swirling around us like a living thing.

The cool night air brushed past their skin, but even it couldn't cool the heat between them—the heat that always burned when they spoke truths they didn't want to hear.

"Tell me something, Cash," Tru said, her voice soft but firm, cutting through the night like a blade. She had a way of cutting through my defenses that no one else could.

"You ever think about the damage all this is doing to your soul?"

The question had me almost speechless. And I nearly yielded to the urge of pushing her away, to protect my pride. But I knew I couldn't because she was right.

"You think I don't?" I finally said, my voice rough with a mixture of anger and regret.

"The damage is the price of admission, Tru. You know that."

"But I ain't got no choice. This is how the game is played."

She let out a long breath, staring out over the city skyline as if the answers were somewhere out there. The neon glow from downtown seemed to mock the aura of quiet desperation.

"You're so full of contradictions, Cash. One minute you're quoting scripture, and the next, you're out here living like the devil's apprentice. You can't have it both ways. You wanna walk with saints, but you're always staring at the guns."

I shifted, because Tru was uncomfortable with her words, but not enough to deny them.

"I don't want to walk with saints, Tru. Hell, I don't even know what that means anymore. I'm just trying to survive out here."

I was trying to sound hard, but the lie tasted like dirty rags.

As she turned to me, her eyes sharp but filled with something else—something that was close to pity, but not quite.

"Surviving doesn't mean living, Cash. It's just existing. And you're better than that."

And I wanted to believe it, but all I saw were broken dreams, torn pages, and possibilities. The truth was a sudden, powerful nuisance.

Better than that? Maybe in some world, but not in this one.

My mind flashed back to the lyrics on my latest mixtape, the one that dropped last week. I rapped about the trap, my experiences hustling, and the false gods I worshipped in the streets.

But as I spit bars, something darker, more real than I ever intended. My raps were about angels holding pistols, about saints with gold teeth.

Painted religious imagery over violent memories, using music to process the shame that had been eating me alive. And I crossed the line from being conceited to shedding layers.

"I use the music to deal with it," Cashmere said, his voice quiet now, almost distant. "I turn it into something. Something I can own. The pain... the survival... it's all in the lyrics."

Tru raised an eyebrow. "The music's the only place you get to speak the truth, huh?"

"It's the only place that doesn't try to save me. I don't need saving, Tru. I need something that makes sense of this."

She sighed. "Then make sense of it, Cash. Stop running from what you feel. Stop wrapping yourself in the mask of the game, pretending like it's all you got."

But I didn't know how to respond. I was caught in the middle of two identities, two gospels that were never aligned. The streets told me loyalty was everything, and respect was earned. While the church told me that I had to forgive just to be free.

Yet, each time I tried, the only thing I ended up with was a deeper hole in my soul. I had to grow past the trap.

Would I let the world define who I am?

As the night stretched on, Tru sat there beside me, her silence more comforting than any words she could offer. We understood how unyielding the game was and the burden of survival tested us more than any sermon.

The **mixtapes kept coming,** each one darker than the last, each verse a prayer for redemption. I was building my own cathedral, brick by painful brick, based on lyrics and regret.

The streets had a way of stealing your soul. And I had let it take more than I cared to admit.

SIDE B - BEAUTIFUL CHAOS: Active & Aesthetic

Love, ego, and trauma.

Track 5: Ladies Love Cashmere

"When we first touched... I felt her....
Cinnamon. Soulful. Euphoria.
Silky & warm. Like she had been there – 4 a lifetime

Waiting 4 me 2 notice.
Tru Skyye was amazing. When she entered a room... She claimed it.
Graceful. Seductive aura. Passion in her eyes."

It had been years since I had been to the city. Life was different after I moved away. But it was the only way that I knew to survive the trap where I was born.

So, I decided to get outside for the night. Maybe see what ladies I could add to the roster. But it didn't go as I expected.

I saw the baddest thing that I had ever seen. Couldn't believe it at first.

But it was something about the way she stood there.

The way she titled her head.

Something new. Refreshing. Yet also, familiar. As if, we met in another lifetime.

We were at a local art show, but it wasn't the art that pulled me in—it was her. She was standing by a sculpture, completely engrossed in it, her dark curls framing her face like they were part of the masterpiece.

I stared at her for a few moments, my mind racing in many directions.

Could it be her?

No way? Does she remember me?

Tru Skyye…

I'd be lying if I said it didn't fit her perfectly.

I hadn't seen her since we were younger, so there were some things that changed. But she was even more of a force, a presence, one that grabbed you by the collar and demanded attention without even trying.

Beyond beautiful.

She was a glitch in the chaotic matrix of my life—a sudden, beautiful pause.

She had this way of making the space around her feel smaller, like everything else just faded away. I don't even know if she noticed me walking toward her.

But I noticed her. God, did I notice her.

Her eyes weren't just looking at the sculpture—they were reading it, like she could see layers the artist had buried beneath the surface. I wanted to know what she saw, to dive into that mystery of hers. But

I was too busy pretending I cared about the abstract metal monstrosity she was staring at.

Truth was, I wasn't here for art. I was here for her. I was here to unpack her quiet intensity and figure out how to consume it.

It's funny, really. I'm a man who's been through the dirt, seen too much to get caught up in the subtle things. But she wasn't like the women I knew. She wasn't like anyone I'd ever met. When she finally spoke, her voice was soft—like velvet brushing against bare skin.

"Layers are always there… even in silence."

I don't know why, but that hit me. Right in the chest. Like the weight of it sank down deep into me, tucked into corners I didn't know existed. It wasn't just a line.

It was *her*.

"Tru….?"

"It's me! David."

Her eyes widened, a small gasp escaping her lips when she finally recognized me.

"David?!! David Cashmere?!!"

The moment my arms closed around her, the familiar scent of her skin was everything I needed.

She looked at me the same way as when we were younger.

It had been over a decade. And we weren't those same kids anymore. Bright eyes and big dreams we used to have.

But right before my eyes, the girl I used to know was gone. She was a new woman who could change the entire world.

It was the way she carried herself, the way she thought. Layers. Yeah, that's exactly what she had. Every word, every glance, was immersed in mystery, yet so real.

I could feel it, all of it.

And just like that, she walked away to another part of the gallery. But I knew that wasn't the end. Her smile held a knowing with her lips, which told me all that I needed to know. She knew the effect she had on me. And I couldn't leave without her.

Ain't no way I was letting this go. Not tonight. So, I made my move. We exchanged numbers and I went my way.

Then, the next day, I texted her to see if she would meet me. When I saw her, I gave her a lavender cashmere sweater that I saw in a store in the city. This was more than a gift. It was soft and delicate, something you could wear like a second skin, and hold onto without needing to touch.

That's how she felt to me—like something I could possess without ever fully understanding. Sometimes that's how life goes, people change. And time can either grow or suppress us.

But the smooth and warm touch of cashmere reminded me of her. Of that moment. I needed her to know that I am a new man.

In hopes it would cover the scars I felt on the inside.

She didn't speak when she opened it, just held it to her chest for a second. There was something in her eyes, a fusion of curiosity and compassion. I saw her not as an enigma, but as a woman, raw and real. Her softness matched the sweater, because I knew there was strength at the core. That's the thing about cashmere, of course it's very fragile, but also resilient.

That's how I felt around her: *fragile*, but ready to come together again.

The days that followed blended together, fueled by layers of conversation. We shared special moments that were placed together like an abstract collage. No straight lines between us. It was all intricate pieces of memories, rebuilding the time we lost. But her thoughts, along with my thoughts collided together, creating something uniquely beautiful.

We spent hours creating art, collages, shooting short films. Even filming spoken word pieces over the top of Marvin Gaye samples. Her voice, soft and sweet, became my soundtrack to everything.

Her spoken word didn't sound like poetry, more like *coded confessions*. And I was the only one who held the key.

But it wasn't just the art that had me enticed by her. It was how she understood me like no one else ever had. No one else could capture me in a delicate mystery. And make a smile feel like the most peaceful place on earth.

We had our own rhythm, our own language. Maybe that's what it was; the way our hearts beat in sync when we were together. Even if we weren't saying anything at all, our silence was a dialect spoken only by two survivors.

But love, like cashmere, was never simple. I knew it. She knew it. The tenderness between us was tangible, with each touch, every conversation could stretch until it snapped. There was always the feeling that something could unravel at any moment. Still, I couldn't walk away. Not when she felt like that sweater—soft, vulnerable, but capable of holding more than I ever could imagine.

That feeling stayed with me, burned into my chest. It wasn't just art. It wasn't just sex. She was something more. She was everything I'd been looking for, wrapped in a mystery I couldn't unravel. She was the piece I didn't know I needed.

In that moment, I knew this was the beginning. Not just of us, but of something much bigger—something deeper than art, deeper than love. Something that would change both of us forever.

And like I always said, ladies love cashmere.

But I didn't care about any of that. All I cared about was the next time I could hold her in my arms without ever touching her. I wanted to consume her completely but settle for the tension of needing her space.

The days bled into nights, and every second with Tru felt like the pause between breaths—like time had forgotten how to move when we were in the same room. I remember the first time we stayed up, talking, no agenda, no rush.

Just us, sitting in my studio while the sound of an old soul samples and records playing low in the background, the needle scratching softly on the vinyl. We didn't need to speak much, but we talked about everything.

She had this way of talking that made me listen harder, as if every word came with a weight that I couldn't ignore. I wasn't used to that. My life had been loud, full of noise. The streets were loud. The struggles were loud.

Even my dreams had been loud, pushing me to prove something, to rise above it all. But with Tru, it wasn't about proving anything. She didn't demand my attention. She just took it, and for the first time in a long while, I wasn't trying to escape the weight of the world. With her, the world felt lighter.

She said things like, "Sometimes silence is louder than words." And I'd feel the tremor of it, that deep knowing that settled in my chest. She'd say it like she wasn't teaching me but showing me something I already knew but had forgotten.

In her eyes, I could see every lesson I'd ever been taught, every truth I'd buried, all of it coming to the surface in the quiet spaces between us.

Her gaze was an unforgiving spotlight, and I couldn't look away from my own reflection.

We'd spend hours on our art projects, creating photo collages, weaving stories into the frames. She'd sit close, her fingers grazing over old photos and Polaroids, pressing them into place with a tenderness that made me ache.

When she did speak, it was always to add something raw, something beautiful. She saw the world in a way I never had, piecing together the chaos and finding meaning in the mess.

One night, we worked through the early hours of the morning, making something that felt like magic, something more than just art. We had a rhythm when we worked—her fingers brushing against mine as we cut, glued, arranged the pieces. There was something about how her presence matched every move I made.

I didn't need to speak to feel heard. She could see the puzzle I was trying to piece together. We didn't need explanations. It was art, yes, but it was also us. There was a thread between us, an unspoken understanding, that I couldn't name but could feel vibrating in my chest. The air between us felt thick, like a drug and I was addicted to it.

I remember the first time she leaned into me, her breath hot on my neck as she whispered, "We're making a story of us, you know."

I couldn't respond right away. There was a part of me that was still scared of what she was saying, scared of what it meant.

But when I looked at her, all my fears faded into the background, drowned by the way her lips curled up into a smile, the way her eyes held mine like they knew the truth even before I could admit it to myself.

She was both muse and mirror.

In her, I saw everything I had been running from—and everything I wanted to be. But even that was fragile. Love like that—it stretches, it bends, it challenges you in ways you can't imagine.

I was no stranger to that kind of tension. Hell, I had grown up with it. But this? This felt different.

It wasn't long before we started filming those spoken word videos. She'd write a poem, and I'd shoot the visuals, playing with light and shadow, creating something as intangible as the way she made me feel.

Her voice, low and smooth, dripped with the kind of sorrow and sweetness I couldn't describe. It made the words heavy. It made the silence between the lines thicker, fuller.

Her desolation was a deep, intoxicating well that I found myself wanting to be absorbed within.

We'd watch the footage, cut and recut, our eyes meeting across the room, sharing a moment of quiet acknowledgment.

There was a tension in the air that I could almost touch, something pulling me closer to her. I didn't know if it was the art we were making or the way she moved—like she wasn't just creating a vision, she was shaping the space around us into something sacred, something only we could understand.

But what scared me was that I could feel myself unraveling. Every time she said something, every time we shared another quiet moment, it felt like she was getting under my skin. She wasn't just inspiring me. She was transforming me. And I wasn't sure if I was ready for that kind of change.

The nights were the worst. I'd wake up, thinking about her, and I couldn't shake the feeling that we were walking a fine line.

Cashmere soft and fragile, yes, but also stronger than most people could ever understand.

Love like that—the kind that wraps around you, gentle but heavy—could hold you together or tear you apart. And I knew, deep down, that Tru and I, we were playing with fire.

There were pieces of me I wasn't ready to show her, pieces of my past that I buried so deep even I couldn't find them. But somehow, with Tru, I didn't feel the need to hide. She made me feel seen, and I didn't know if that was a gift or a curse.

There were nights when she'd show up in that lavender cashmere sweater, her scent mingling with the fabric.

The way she wore it, it was like she was wrapped in more than just softness—she was wrapped in something else too. Something I couldn't put my finger on. Every time she looked at me, it was like she could see me—not just the man everyone thought I was, but the one I was still trying to figure out. The one who had been buried under layers of past mistakes, of broken promises and shattered dreams.

But Tru, she didn't see the broken parts. She didn't see the pieces that weren't put together yet. She saw me. All of me.

And maybe that was what scared me the most. That I was beginning to need her more than I wanted to admit. Maybe I was starting to unravel, piece by piece, every time I was around her. But if love was like cashmere, fragile and easy to ruin, then maybe it was worth the risk.

Because with her, I felt like I could stretch beyond what I was, beyond the weight of everything that had ever held me down. With her, I was more than a man from the South with a broken past.

I could create and dream.

And damn it, I wanted to keep dreaming with her.

The truth? I didn't know where this would go. I didn't know if we could make it last.

Still, I couldn't walk away from her. She made me feel like I was more than the history of my scars. I had always lived with the understanding that most good things end, especially in a system that wasn't designed for you.

This time, she was different. Even more than what I remember.

For the first time in my life, I only had my eyes and heart focused on one woman. I had to see where this would go. I wanted to see if we could build something real. Something I was never gonna let go.

Like cashmere, love was fragile, but maybe. Just maybe, it was worth holding on, even if it stretched and unraveled.

Track 6: Cry Now, Laugh Later

*"Lead flying through the glass, death whispering my name,
Started bartering with God, my soul bleeding in the rain.*

*Brushes dipped in trauma, painting portraits of the strife,
Now my book of rhymes is the medic, stitching verses back 2 life."*

Can't believe I'm still here?

I didn't expect to make it.

Not after the other night.

It was nonstop gunfire, seemed like outta nowhere. But that happened sometimes so I paid it no mind. But this time it was more rapid than usual, like the universe was tryna take me down.

Was it the sound of my last day? I could hear the bullets ricochetting off the concrete walls.

As usual, I was posted on the block at 5th and Lenox. Really just doing me, minding my own damn business. That's when a bullet pierced the wall behind me.

I turned, checking my surroundings, but that could be aimed at me. *Naw, couldn't be.* It was quiet for a second, but not for long. Then came the blast of the second shot, and it was closer.

The last bullet whizzed by my ear like a whisper of death.

So, I ran and hid behind an old car nearby. Trembling, and hands shaking uncontrollably, I was more scared than I had ever been in my whole life. It was wild because I couldn't see where the fuck the bullets came from. Nothing made any sense.

All kinds of lights. Sirens around me. There were even people close by, but they just turned the other way. What's crazy is that I was alone in a city that once showed me love. It was then, when I realized no one really cared whether I lived or died.

I could taste residue from chemicals in the concrete, reminding me of this cold world.

Then, only thing I knew to do was pray. A voice inside me, quiet but loud enough to stop me in that moment.

God, if you're listening. I need you now. *Have mercy on me... please help me.*

I didn't stop for an answer. Still I asked anyway, even though I wasn't sure what would happen. Being so close to death, I was willing to try anything. I was thirsty for something, I needed to believe in the impossible. I demanded to see a sign that was not the end for me.

Then, there was a third shot that came much faster than the rest. But my instincts kicked in, almost like God had sent protection for me to react in time. My face hit the ground, slamming my chest against the street. I knew someone was tryna kill me.

Gasping for air, I felt like a caged animal trapped.

My eyes closed. For a second that felt like hours.

But I refused to let death come visit me. For a few moments... nothing. I didn't hear any more shots. Only the pain of silence.

Then, I felt the courage to open my eyes. I didn't see anyone.

What happened, was the person shooting gone? Or was this God giving me another chance? I don't know but after this my perception of life changed.

I was afraid in the moment. But then, I became numb. There was a cold emptiness because I didn't have time to feel anything else.

All I knew to do was get back on my feet. My heart was pounding a million miles a minute, and blood was in my eyes and ears. But I knew this wasn't the end. Not yet.

Later, when I found my way back to my studio, I did something I'd never done before. I picked up a paintbrush, dirty with leftover oils from some project I'd been too tired to finish, and I started to paint.

I didn't know what I was doing. I didn't know why I was doing it.

All I knew was I had to get the feeling out of me—the anger, the terror, the emptiness. It had been building up, and now it had to be somewhere. Not in my soul, not in my body. It needed to leave, because if I didn't, I was gonna collapse.

I started with reds and blacks, heavy strokes that felt like punches, like the way the world had hit me and kept hitting me. And as the brush met the canvas, I could feel the weight of everything—my past, the streets, the drugs, the deals, the pain, the betrayals, the endless nights of fighting to stay above water. Every color, every streak, every drop was me, showing up in a way I had never dared to. I was angry. I was hurting.

And for the first time, I realized I didn't need to hold it all in anymore. The world had been trying to break me for years, but I was still standing. The canvas was my screaming therapy session, and the paint, my spilled guts.

After the paint dried on the canvas, I stepped back. It wasn't art. It was survival. That's what I'd made: survival. I didn't care about beauty. I didn't care about perfection. This was just me letting the world know that I wasn't done yet.

When the sun went down, I grabbed a pen and sat at the desk, feeling like I was about to explode from the inside. I didn't pick up the mic that night. No, I didn't need the mic. I needed something raw, something real.

I grabbed a notebook, and I started writing. At first, it wasn't even rap. It was just me talking to myself, trying to make sense of everything I was feeling. But that's how it always starts, right? You don't realize you're rapping until you're already rapping.

"Cry now, laugh later"—shit, **that's the motto.**

Tears ain't for me. Not anymore.

I grew up in the gutter, where crying gets you dead or forgotten, but damn, I wasn't trying to be either. So, I started writing it out—lines about the struggle, the pain, the losses. Every verse, every hook became a note to myself, a reminder that I had survived, I was surviving, and I would keep surviving.

I wrote about the nights when the streets felt like a trap. Then, about the women who had left me broken. Even about the homies who had betrayed me, and the ones I'd lost along the way. But more than anything, I wrote about the moments when I thought I couldn't make it.

This time, I didn't spend time thinking. But I continued to write until the ink ran out on my paper.

This wasn't just music. It was my life. My release therapy.

My lyrics came out raw, filled with the exact pain and emotion that I put on canvas. Every sixteen bars (verse) was another step forward. Didn't matter if the world ever heard, or if it went platinum. What mattered was that I was still here. And every bar, every verse, every beat was proof that I survived.

I sat back, lit my blunt, then the smoke filled my lungs. Then, the voice in my head said….

"Cry now, laugh later."

That was the key to survival. That was what the streets had taught me. You break down, you fall apart, but you don't stay there. You get up. You smile later, when the storm clears and you're still standing.

But there was something else now, something new. I wasn't just surviving anymore. I was fighting to live. And I didn't know what that fight would cost me, but I was ready. I was always ready.

And so, I spit bars from my soul.

Lyrics for the dead. Lyrics for the broken.

I spit for the ones who were still out there, trying to make it out the mud. But most of all, I spit those bars for me. For David Cashmere.

The one who didn't just survive but rose every time the world tried to knock him down.

Cry now, laugh later.

The next day, I didn't tell anyone about the shooting. Didn't make sense to talk about something that life altering. Just move past it and keep going, like it's another day. But the truth was, it stayed with me each day after it happened.

When the night came there was a shift inside of me. Funny thing, these streets don't give you reflection time. Either you are moving forward or the past keeps you standing still. But I was gonna let that be my reality.

I didn't call Tru. Not at first. I really didn't wanna scare her. Didn't want her thinking I was some broken man who needed saving. I'd always prided myself on being the one people leaned on. The one who handled shit. But this time, it was different. This time, I wasn't sure how to handle it.

I wasn't sure how to handle me. My mask felt heavy and cracked, and she was the only one who could **see the fear beneath**.

But by midday, I found myself on the phone, dialing her number.

The phone rang twice before she picked up. Her voice was soft, like always, but I could hear the concern in it.

"You good?" she asked, no hesitation. She always knew when something was off.

She didn't ask *what's wrong*, she asked *are you whole*?

"Yeah," I lied, running a hand through my hair. "Just... got caught up in some shit last night. But I'm straight."

I could hear her exhale on the other side. "David, what happened?"

I hesitated. I wasn't ready to tell her the full story. Hell, I wasn't even sure I wanted to talk about it. But Tru didn't let shit slide. She knew when something was eating at me.

"Just... some random shots. Ain't nothing to a real one?" I said, making light of the situation.

"You're lying," she snapped. "I know you, David. Talk to me. What happened?"

I cursed under my breath. "I got shot at, Tru. Damn?!"

Nothing. A long pause. I could hear a strong sigh on the other end of the phone. She was fueled with mixed emotions of anger and concern. It bothered me because I never wanted to put her in that position. It was all my fault. I was the one acting as if I was untouchable.

"God, David..." Her voice was trembling now, but wouldn't let go of me. "Do you know what's happening? Cash, you can't live like this. You're not bulletproof."

I laughed casually. "Bulletproof? No way. I'm just doing what I gotta do out here. Ain't no fairy tale for me."

"I'm serious," she shot back.

"You're running, David. Running from yourself, from everything. You think art and mixtapes gonna change this? You're gonna be gone soon if you keep it up. You're playing with fire, but too damn stubborn to see it."

Feeling the *fear of her voice* was more alarming than any bullet.

I wasn't ready to hear that. I didn't want to hear that. But she was right.

"Well, fire is all good with me," I muttered, staring out the window of my apartment. "That's what keeps me alive. Without that pressure, I'm nothing."

"Bullshit," she fired off at me. "You think it's pressure that keeps you alive? You're afraid. Afraid to have something better. Too scared to leave the streets because you don't know anything else."

I took a moment of silence because I wanted to hang up. But again, like always, she was right. Still my pride got the best of me, and I needed to be alone.

"I gotta go, Tru," I said, in a low tone. "I'll talk to you later."

Then, I just hung up the phone.

……She knew. I wasn't ready to be saved. The only thing I knew to do was run.

Track 7: Life Goes On, Barely

"Motel walls closing in, darkness dancing with the end,
Until a flicker in the soul forced my broken heart 2 mend.

In the silence of the couch, therapy felt like a cage,
Till I turned my freestyle hymns into scriptures on a page."

When I got a room at the motel, I checked-in under another name. Where I'm from fake ID's were a regular part of the game. Most of the time, you probably didn't even know the name on there. And right now, being me was too heavy. All I needed was somewhere quiet to get out of my own head.

This room smelled like spoiled food and nightmares.

Holes and burns in a damp comforter.

The one thing that stood out was the Bible in the drawer. And you could tell that no one had ever read or touched it. *Tonight, wouldn't be any different.*

As I sat on the end of the bed, I turned to look at my strap on the nightstand. It wasn't much but my old faithful, and reliable .38 special. So, many times it protected me and never let me down.

Some moments in life are full circle.

Maybe one. Just one bullet. Then, I closed my eyes.

Heart racing. Click.

I'm still here?

Driving by the motel that night, outside, you could see the **VACANCY** sign flashing repeatedly. But inside, the room was dark, and my world was crashing down.

I knew that I needed to pray but couldn't find the words. All I could do was ask…

"God… can you hear me?! I need help!"

Nothing.

"So, you're just watching me go through pain?! I can't do this!!"

Quiet. The only sounds were from the dusty air conditioner, and my spirit telling me not to give up.

Then, I thought about Tru.

My homies from the neighborhood.

Mama's voice singing and praying early in the morning. I could visualize my unborn son, who was just a dream. But the problem was that I got tired. And I was tired of being tired.

Second time.

Pushed the chrome to my head.
Closed my eyes, again.

Alone in the darkness. I woke up.

And I started feeling the weight of everything. The mistakes that I made, sleepless nights.

Then, I started to see my whole life flashing before my eyes.

Tears filled my eyes. And ran down my face, rivers overflowing. It was an ugly cry.

I threw my gun as hard as I could across the room.

If I wasn't gonna die that night. I had to let *the old me* go.

The next morning, I checked myself into therapy. Not rehab. Not church. **Therapy.**

They gave me a clipboard full of forms, and a woman named **Dr. Lewis** with the kind of calm that made me suspicious. She spoke soft, moved slow, like she was scared to scare me.

"Tell me why you're here, David," she said, folding her hands in her lap.

I stared at the floor. "I ain't sure I am."

She waited. Didn't push. Just let the silence sit between us like an unwelcome guest. Finally, I sighed.

"You ever been so numb you start missing pain?"

She nodded; eyes locked on mine. "Every day I listen to people who feel that way. You're not alone."

I laughed, sharp and dry. "Feels like it."

Therapy was weird. Silence felt like a foreign language.

Every time she asked a question, I felt like I was peeling back a layer I didn't want to see. But somewhere between the awkward pauses and the tears I tried to hide, something started shifting.

She said, "You've been **surviving** for so long, David. You ever thought about *what living might look like*?"

That question haunted me more than the bullets ever did.

I started filling my notebooks again. Not just with rhymes—scripture. Words that weren't meant to flex, but to *heal*.

Every freestyle became a hymn. Every sketch became a prayer.

Late nights, I'd sit by my window, pencil in one hand, blunt in the other, sketching faces I'd seen in dreams—faces I'd loved, faces I'd lost. Each one had a halo of chaos around it. I didn't even notice until Dr. Lewis pointed it out.

"You keep drawing halos," she said one day. "Why?"

I shrugged. "Maybe I'm just trying to remember what light looks like."

Life didn't get easier after that. It never does. But it *did* start moving again. Slowly. Barely. Like an old record skipping on the turntable but still managing to play the song.

I started showing up. To therapy. To life. Even to myself.

Tru came back around, cautious but curious. My homie, Marcus, hit me up, said he heard the new track I'd dropped online—*Cry Now, Smile Later (Remix)*—and said, "Damn, Cash, you sound alive for the first time in forever."

Maybe he was right. Maybe I was.

Because that's the thing about life—it doesn't stop when you want it to. It drags you, bruised and breathless, back to the surface.

And me? I ain't perfect. I still wake up some days feeling like the gun's in my hand. But then I look at the light creeping through the blinds, the paint stains on my fingers, the notebooks full of verses that sound like resurrection—

—and I remember:

I didn't die in that motel.

I was reborn in it.

Life goes on.
Barely.
But it goes.

I walked into the studio late that night, the weight of the world still pressed against my chest, but this time, I could breathe through it. I could still feel the darkness clinging to me, like a shadow that wouldn't let go, but it was quieter now.

Less suffocating.

The moment I sat down at the mic, it hit me. This was it. The one thing that never judged me, never tried to fix me, never expected me to be anything other than raw. The music was my only real therapy.

I laid down a few bars, and then a few more. The beat kept building. My voice wasn't just words anymore. It was a cry. A prayer. A promise to never go back to that motel room.

"If I die tonight, let it be in rhythm, let my last breath be a beat."

I stopped and listened to it play back. The words had been born in that silence, that darkness, but now they were something else—something alive. And maybe that's what life is. It's not about avoiding the pain or pretending it doesn't exist. It's about using it. Turning it into something real. Something worth breathing for.

Marcus called me up a few days later, told me the track was getting mad traction. "Man, you're *buzzing*, Cash. People feeling that rawness in your voice. They hear the struggle in it."

I didn't care about the buzz. I didn't care if it went platinum. What mattered was that *I* felt it. I was alive in the music, and maybe for the first time, I was starting to feel alive in my own skin too.

Dr. Lewis kept pushing me, but it wasn't just her. It was Tru. It was Marcus. It was the people who still saw something in me, even when I didn't. I had to face all those things I'd been avoiding—the ghosts, the guilt, the anger—and start making peace with it. Start making *music* out of it.

A week later, Tru showed up at my door, knocking softly like she wasn't sure if she had a right to be there. But she did. She always did.

She didn't say much. Just looked at me, then looked at the canvas I'd been working on. She was smart enough to read between the lines. To see what wasn't being said.

"How you doing?" she asked, because she knew what I was feeling.

"I'm doing better."

A few days after that, I knew it was time for me to be raw, real, and true to myself.

Like it had been waiting to be spoken. Like it had been there all along, hidden under layers of regret.

"Born outta struggle, raised up in pain,
Now I'm pushin' 4 freedom, tryna escape the darkness and rain."

Not perfect. Kinda rusty. But real. Me.

That was it.

Life goes on, barely. But it goes.

Track 8: Do Ya Feel Me?

"Burning out from the heat, battling the demons in my head,
Using this canvas as a bridge sayin' things I never said.
Clean Hands on vinyl, audio visuals for scars,
Giving purpose to the youth's showin' soul beyond these bars."

Often, I think to myself: *How did I really make it this far?* This is bigger than the bullets aimed at me that missed, or the dirty game of the streets. There were times when I was mentally unstable. And I knew that I was running from something, but wasn't really sure what I was running toward.

Now it's clear why they call it the trap. The streets, this cycle that I grew up in is definitely that. But life can feel that way too because the fall is inevitable, no matter who you are.

So, I was tired. And even feeling burnout. I needed to recharge myself.

Sleepless nights, consistent anxiety was my daily normal. Many days, I would wake up in a cold sweat, having flashbacks of the streets. Seemed like no matter how much music or art that I created, the pain was still there. Even without sold shows, there was an emptiness living inside me.

So, I decided to paint more often, not only as a distraction, but also to serve as a therapy. This was one way to keep my mind as free and clear as possible. Sometimes, I would just throw different colors of paint on the canvas. Splashing colors all over the place. Red was the pain. Black was the grief. Blue was the depths of my unspoken soul.

The technique or talent that I had no longer made a difference.

Just creating. No structure. No plan. My life started to make more sense through my ability to create.

Years full of trauma. Bad decisions.

Everything was there on canvas.

One night, I finished an abstract piece that looked like a landscape of scars. Bold colors, sharp lines. Sorta like a beautiful struggle.

Standing there proud, looking at the finished product, I decided to capture the moment. I took a picture, and I posted it online. Not planned, just being in the moment.

A few minutes later, my post went viral. And I received hundreds of messages from people who saw themselves through my work.

That's when it hit me: I'm not alone in this battle.

Then, I knew I had to do a pop-up art show. It was called *Painted Pain*. My art, album covers. A total collage that reflected my hustle, struggle, and adversity that I had made it through. Every painting was a snippet outta my life: forgotten dreams, hidden truths, and raw emotion.

My audience was the youth. That's right! Kids. Many times, it's the young children that have been put to the back, forgotten. So, they needed to see something real. Just like me.

The night of the gallery, there were so many people there it was hard for me to process it. People were connected to each painting like it said something to them. Almost like everyone came in search of something, and they found it in my work.

The air had an aroma of liberation, a new rejuvenated energy that was never in my city. Even in the silence of people viewing the art. I could hear: *Yeah, I feel you*.

Man. It was heavy in that moment. Not just my pain, but the weight of their pain. I could feel all of it. Everything. This was what I needed.

The connection. The community.

After the pop-up, I started working on my concept album, called *Clean Hands*. This was not about being "clean", or without flaws, but accepting and owning it all. Never, had I shown the courage to not run from who I was. I wasn't a hero. Or even a villain. But I was a young black man who wanted to write my wrongs, one track at a time.

I finished my album faster than I initially thought. The tracks were hard, vivid, but more personal. Every track was a visual, a snapshot, a story. Then, to enhance the experience, I created artwork to capture the essence of each song. *Clean Hands* wasn't just music—it was a journey, a roadmap through the mess. This wasn't an album for me, but strictly for my fans. The ones that supported me from day one.

I hit up a few people from the neighborhood, to help expand my reach. Some of these people might have seen me as just a rapper. That didn't matter. But what did matter was making sure there were more voices that could speak to the youth.

I put my hands all over this project: writing, producing, and recording. Because I knew that I had to get dirty in order for it to come out clean. Similar to the story of my life. No shiny suit music. This was bold, vivid from the core. The visuals were very gritty and dark, unapologetic. This was a reflection of my world.

I remember the day that the album dropped. The streams, comments, and likes didn't really cross my mind much. Numbers only told part of the story. It was time to write a new narrative. A new normal. The accolades and awards were not the objective this time.

Did I reach the people? Did they feel me?

That's what mattered. I was finally speaking to the ones who needed it the most. Those feeling defeated, still searching for a way out.

In a few moments of silence, I realized that this was a turning point. A pivot. Not music. This was a movement. My message was finally reaching the youth. The goal was to show them they weren't alone.

This was a purpose bigger than applause.

The movement began to grow.

Started calling my youth audience, the young ones. They were super dope. Supporting the movement and all of my shows, pop-ups. We had some very deep, authentic conversations. It wasn't just about music, but real life too. The things that were hidden, secret. Things haunting our peace, and made most wanna give up.

It was time to put more ideas in motion. So, I started hosting workshops, working mostly with kids from the same environments that I came from. We discussed everything. Art. Music. Mental Health. The objective was to let their voices be heard in a major way. Showing them how to turn pain into power, and fuel that power with purpose.

When I saw the glimpse of hope in their eyes, it made me believe that we had to keep going.

We were becoming one. Not just preaching to them. I was speaking *with* them. This was the part of my calling that I didn't know existed. Knowing that I could reach them, It wasn't the applause that energized me. It was amazing to see the lives that I impacted.

A bridge between the struggle and the healing. This was the bridge that was being created. This was keeping me alive. I needed it.

But I kept going, and didn't stop. I painted. I wrote. I showed up. Consistently.

So……every time they ask me: *Do ya feel me?*

Yeah, lil homie I do. And I always will.

RECORD II - THE ASCENSION YEARS:

Turning pain into power and policy.

SIDE C - CLEAN HANDS: Awakening & Purpose

Healing and creating something bigger.

Track 9: Trap Ain't a Place, It's a Cycle

"New city, new lens, opening the gallery doors,
Teaching tech and how 2 hustle, gotta get what's
yours

At war with the government, fighting zoning and the
gate,
Using strategy and fortitude 2 circumvent the hate."

Some might think of the trap as a place, street corner, or even maybe a block.

But nah. The trap ain't a place. Worse than that. It's a cycle. Just a hamster wheel holding you hostage, without a way to escape. Shit, what's crazy is that's not the worst part. At a certain point, you start thinking your only option is to stay there. It ain't about no bricks and bars. It is a cage, mental prison where you must balance choices versus your *survival*.

They got us believing we are meant to only just get by, not truly live. Our whole lives this philosophy has a claim on our soul. That's the *real* trap.

But guess what? This cycle wasn't gonna get me. Fuck being another statistic, news headline, or social media hashtag. So, I decided to swing back at **the system.**

I knew if I was ever gonna *break the cycle*, it was time to create my own.

I opened the studio and gallery in a new city, a place with fresh streets but the same old battles. The goal of all this was making permanent *change*. So, I found a spot in a different part of the city that really needed help. No one ever went back to this neighborhood once they left.

But I was gonna change that.

On the outside it just looked like an old warehouse near downtown. Although, it appeared that way the building and area spoke to me.

The type of place people drove past without giving it a second look. But I could feel the history, and untold stories the walls would tell if you listened hard enough. So, I put everything I had into it. Blood, sweat, and tears into fixing it up.

The first time I walked inside, the place was empty. Floors were dirty, windows broken, and graffiti all over the place. Still, I saw a blank canvas of opportunity.

All types of visual artists came to help: painters, sculptors, graphic artists. Basically, every single type of creator, just like me. We put art on every surface of the building.

I wanted you to feel the heartbeat when you entered. This was gonna be the new pulse of creativity. A new vibration that transcended beyond struggle or survival.

Not just another art gallery. A cultural experience.

Here you could escape, and free your mind. There would be no negative energy. I called it *Rebirth Studio*. This would be the genesis of art therapy for the community.

A place to create something new. A place where the trap didn't exist.

I wasn't just putting up paintings and sculptures. I was putting up a whole new narrative. One that included people who had never been given the chance to write their own stories. This wasn't about selling paintings for big checks; this was about *building*.

I didn't just want to make art for the rich folks who'd hang it on their walls and forget it existed by the end of the week. I wanted to reach the ones who never thought they could be part of that world—the ones who were stuck, trapped in a cycle of poverty and despair.

So, I started something new. I set up tech classes. Artificial intelligence, coding, design, quantum, as well as video and music production. Things that would give kids from the neighborhood a real future.

They were ready and excited to learn something new. Especially when they realized that they could use it with social media and music. I established the program for more than kids. It was for anyone in the neighborhood that wanted to learn.

This was an investment into their life taking a new path. Something that no one else wanted our people to have in their skillset.

One of the first kids I worked with was Malik. At 16 yrs old he was kinda tall, and you could tell he had seen too much already.

He was slick, with a street-smart aura. Yet beneath everything, I could see fear. There was a hunger for survival in his eyes.

"Yo, Cash," he said one day, hands stuffed in his hoodie pocket.

"Can I make money off this shit? For real, I'm just tryna to get paid, you feel me?"

I leaned back in my chair, watching him. I didn't answer right away. As I watched his face, silence filled the room.

Finally, I said, "Yeah, you can. But it's about more than money. This gives you **control**. Understanding technology, software, hardware, and artificial intelligence puts you in the game. You're becoming a boss."

He was silent. And continued watching the screen, like he didn't believe that he belonged. But I wasn't gonna let him fall back into the cycle.

"Look, Malik," I said, while pointing to the painting of a broken chain.

"We are breaking the cycle. Ain't nobody else gonna break it for you. It's on us. This is our birth right. This is freedom, but it won't be cheap. We gotta be willing to pay for it."

He stayed quiet, but I could see the wheels turning in his head. That was all I needed.

My focus was on the entire community. But the kids were the key to the future. Yet I knew that this system would let me do this easily.

As soon as I started creating programs, I got major push back. Local government officials, planning and economic development departments, and others did everything to stop me. They establish redevelopment plans, and even zoning laws, without true community engagement. No input from people like us.

They wanna keep you boxed in and stuck in the trap.

But I wasn't designed to be in any box.

Hell, I wasn't born to ever fit in it.

It was exactly what I had expected. The first time I went down to City Hall to fight those zoning laws, and they did everything to shut down my plans.

But they had no idea what they were dealing with.

"Mr. Cashmere," one of the council members said in a condescending tone.

"Do you actually understand the issues with your project? This goes beyond zoning. It's about safety. The priority is protecting the neighborhood."

I look directly in his eyes with a calm intensity.

"Trust me, I understand more than you believe. I get it, you want to keep people like me down. You see those in the hood without access and opportunity. Keep bringing us down."

He was so uncomfortable, but couldn't look away.

"Y'all talk about safety?!" I said with more authority. "But we need equity. If you wanna *see change*? Let us **create** it."

Instead of waiting for the fight to come my way, I initiated it. They tried to push the law at me, but I just turnt up. Kept pushing harder towards the goal. There wasn't anything that was gonna stop us. And they knew it.

This was more than a gallery. It was evolution. This wasn't about money or status. Now the people were in the position of power to change the narrative. They could finally break the cycle.

You feel me? I ain't talking about a place.

This is a cycle.

But if you break it, you can build something else. Something new. Something better. And that's what we're doing.

Building a future that belongs to the ones who create it.

Track 10: Hustlin'

"Deep in Soul Vibes, we saw real music and art come 2 life,
Turned old pews into a stage 2 lead kids to the light.

Out the Mud on the walls, reimaging the South,
Finding peace and healing the heart that's what it's all about."

Hustle.

I love the hustle. Legal or illegal. It's an art form. There are some messages in life that can only be conveyed through this method. The best way to convert struggle into progress.

More than generating a profit, producing a product or manifesting your dreams; it's the art of storytelling. Turning nothin' into something. Taking pieces of nothing to create a whole new reality.

It's transformation, just like transforming lead into gold; we were turning pain into *intellectual profit*.

And where I'm from that means something.

But I wasn't done yet. This was just the surface.

Now it was time to take it higher, elevate the grind. Hustle harder. The city needed something that would last, endure the test of time. No one could deny it. We needed a space to freely release our creativity and passion. This was a place that I would call a home for the soul.

Riding around one day, I saw this super old church downtown. It looked like it had been abandoned for years, maybe even decades. There were busted windows, structural damage to the exterior, and the weeds had outgrown the brown grass. But I also noticed the stained-glass windows, holding some faded beauty. Almost like they were waiting for a fresh breath of air to enter. The building was dying, and I was here to bring it back **to life**.

As I walked into the church, I remember smelling decaying wood and dust. It hit me like distant memories that had been buried under too many years of neglect. Every step I took, I heard the floor squeak beneath my feet like the building was moaning from pain.

But this was an opportunity. It was perfect.

I could see the gallery we would put on the walls, a stage to perform music, and workstations for artists. There was so much potential all over the building. It felt like I heard the voices of my ancestors speaking to me. This was now the hub. People would come here from all over to restore, design, and be free.

This was a vessel. A way for God to work through us.

So, I purchased the building.

I spent all the money I had to fix it.

You could say this was a gamble. I'm crazy, or even that I lost my mind. But I wasn't hearing none of that. There was no room or time for uncertainty. The people needed this and their voices needed to be heard.

There were no expectations on the first day we opened. But I did invite the whole city. My young ones, seniors in the community, and a bunch of my homies from the neighborhood. Anyone, and everyone, who needed a place to express to unwind, free their mind.

We called it *Soul Vibes*. That was the best way to describe the feeling in that building. Your soul was gonna catch the vibe and energy in there. It was freedom. No judgment, no dress code. It didn't matter where you came from. There were no limitations. All that mattered was that you allowed yourself to be open and free to create.

We just wanted people to pour out their soul.

The glue to the place was in the music venue. It was more than just a stage, and you could feel the bass in every performance. This was a foundation for the rhythm to be planted in the city. We had local artists, rappers, poets, producers, and DJs bless the stage. Hustle was only part of the equation. You had to bring that soul vibe.

Then came the workshops. The kids had the opportunity to tell their stories in a unique way. No longer were they ignored or overlooked. Now they were heard on a big scale. The purpose was to help them realize their stories and experiences were worth telling.

This made me start hosting visual storytelling workshops.

"Listen, y'all," I said in front of a group of teens, sitting in the studio with their art supplies, "I understand. Everyone has counted you out, like your story doesn't matter. But this is your time. Your voice counts. Now, you're in position to change your life. Speak from the heart and be yourself, that's all we need from you."

No one said a word.

But a girl named Tyra, about 14 years old, raised her hand. She was a natural born leader, her eyes full of fire. "So, you want us to paint the emotions we got inside?"

"Yes ma'am. It's the only way that we can all be free. The pain that we carry will take over, or it will push you to be better. That's where the power lies, to turn all that hurt into something people can feel."

She thought, then said:

"Ain't nobody asked me how I feel before?"

Smiling, as I replied. "That's the reason for doing this. We gonna make the world listen."

It was cool to see the kids working. Initially, they started out not so sure about what direction to take. But when they began creating, nothing could stop them. Their raw emotion and energy was so contagious. They were evolving right in front of my eyes; from being guarded about opening up, to being fearless enough to tell their stories.

They had discovered their *own unique language*. Speaking from an inner voice, finding **truth beyond words**.

Next, came the exhibit, *Out the Mud: The Dirty South Reimagined*.

It took several months to put it all together. There were paintings, sculptures, poets, and musicians. From the streets to the church. The old neighborhood and all over the city. My whole community, my block was there. This was a statement.

This was a way to redefine what was known as the *"Dirty South"*. There was real stories of morals, values, and principles that we learned being from down here. It actually meant something powerful. This was about culture, strength, and legacy.

The opening event was dope.

The space was full, the music was bumping, and the art was flowing. There was art throughout the building, covering the walls, of stories and dreams ready to be told. Each painting had its own life, speaking from places of brokenness to making it against all odds. And the sculptures carried an aura of resilience that captivated the entire audience.

But there was this one piece that instantly grabbed you as soon as you saw it. It was a shattered whiskey bottle altered in clear resin, which symbolized the ability to sustain beauty in the midst of ruins.

It was cool to see all of the performers on stage too. The spoken word artist and poets spoke to the depths of our beings. Then, the singers came with original songs that were beyond amazing. But it was even more special for me to see the local rappers hit the stage. The whole night was a celebration of a new start, a fresh beginning for our new reality. We didn't have to stay down, it was time to get up.

But the best part?

It was seeing how people reacted. Seeing how they connected with the stories we'd created. The pride that I saw in their eyes made it all worth it. This was the first time I had ever seen some of them smile. But they earned this attention.

The city heard their voice.

Tyra stood proudly, next to her painting. It was a portrait of a woman with her fists raised.

She smiled. Then, I came up to her and said softly.

"Tyra, your story, is gonna change someone's life."

She looked at me with boldness. "I know. It already has."

The exhibition was a success. The art and music resonated with everyone. *Soul Vibes* had now become a place to remember.

The struggle didn't exist within the walls of that building. There was a greater sense of being and pride with all of the creatives involved in the space. We were becoming something greater than ourselves.

This was a feeling better than money could buy. I could see that there was real meaning behind all of this.

Purpose.

Selling paintings was cool and important, but giving to other people hit me hard. The space that we created gave people a new start to renew their minds. This was the very thing the city had been missing all those years. Finally, there was a rose growing from the concrete.

And yeah, I'm still hustlin'. Working nonstop.

Soul Vibes started growing, and it has definitely opened up more opportunities. Still real hustlers know that it ain't about what you keep. The major key was to give something and continue to build while breaking the cycle. We're changing the narrative about The South.

It's always been misunderstood. So, we had to rewrite the story of The South. But, through art, music, and culture at *Soul Vibes* we were on our way to bring a new spirit to the city.

Track 11: The Ballot or the Bullet

"Sirens screaming from nightmares in the dark, pools of blood flooding the concrete,
So, we took back the power, victims 2 murals, ten feet deep

Blending street art with the movement, protest anthems fillin' the air,
Turning culture into body armor for war against a system that ain't fair."

I will never forget the day that my anger came back. It wasn't just because I was having a bad day or moment.

There were a series of moments.

Moments that had built up over years. As I stood, watching my people suffer, die, and go through unnecessary struggle. Even the times we yelled for change, but we were ignored. Then, after the shooting of another young black person it was no longer about watching.

The cold, hard realization that the only difference between me and the victim was the grace and mercy of God……in addition to a skipped heartbeat.

It was time to take action. A shift needed to be created.

A movement.

Now, I'm transitioning into a different game. *Politics.*

I stayed on the sidelines too long. It was time to be the voice for my people. In the past, I hid behind my art, hustle, and being "too busy" to care. Distracted by the studio and performing, trying to make art that related to the people. But, what was the point of it if it didn't speak the truth? If I was gonna keep it real, I had to put my life on the line for my people.

Being neutral was worse than being a coward.

So, I picked up the paintbrush. I picked various shades of colors that pulled at my heart the most: red, black, and yellows. Then, I started to paint. Initially, I didn't know how large the painting would be, but it developed into a mural. A larger than life piece of art in the heart of the city. This was my dedication to the forgotten. A visual wake-up call to raise awareness about us being ignored.

This wasn't just another tragedy. This was a war. But this time we fought strategically with our hearts.

It was a painting of a young black man with his hands raised in civil disobedience. This was not a surrender.

He had a pair of wings that created a dark shadow, because they had been torn away. Then, the background consisted of a dark sky that was immersed in discolorations. As he stood on a foundation of earth was plagued with crushed glass.

"We Are the Resistance." That was the phrase in red painted across the bottom. It was a bold, visual manifesto to say that we were tired.

There was no announcement. No one knew it was coming. This was a message from the future. The next day the entire city saw the truth. It was time to wake up.

As I was painting the next layer, Tru showed up. I didn't expect to see her, but I'm glad she was there. She stood there for a moment, gazing deeply at the mural. There was a quiet desire in her eyes that spoke volumes. It was clear the boldness of the art grabbed her attention.

"What's this?" she asked, I could hear the weight in it.

Looking at her as I wiped my hands and stepping back to stand by her side. "*The message.*"

"The world needs to hear us. It's time to make them listen."

She paused for a second. Her arms crossed. She nodded in agreement. Then, I continued to stay focused on the mural, and I could see the impact it had. Tru never expressed her feelings much in public, but this was clear to see.

"I think you can do more," she said with conviction.

I squinted my eyes in confusion. "You think it's cool to just let it go? Another brother is dead, and nobody is gonna save us?! We have to do something."

She turned to look at me.

"No, but… this gotta show our *humanity*. Not just anger. They can't just take our culture, then use us for hashtags or trends. W**e matter**."

She saw the authenticity I was concealing under my perspective.

And I wasn't sure how to respond to that. She had a point, but right now, all I could do was put my emotions into my art. Still, there was something about her presence that made me question if there was more to do.

"You're right," I agreed, with my voice lower than usual.

"I needed them to see it. The rawness. The violence. They need to feel it deep within."

She stepped closer, tilting her head, studying me like she always did when she was trying to figure out what was really going on.

"What if we gave them a different kind of feeling? What if we used the art to build something, not just tear down everything they've tried to destroy?"

I looked at her, confused. "What do you mean?"

"We need to use this mural as the start of a bigger agenda. Let's get organized and turn art into action. Keep creating the same way, but now there is a purpose. Use our platform, art, and voice, to inspire change. Don't just demand it. Make the change that we want to see."

I was so focused on the protest and being so angry. This was an opportunity to do more than make them feel something. *But maybe Tru was right?* Now, I really started to believe that we could inspire real change and hope.

The next couple of weeks working together, using the urgency of protest with the power of purpose. Tru helped me create an entire campaign around the mural.

Then, made music and visual projects with other activists and collectives. This was our way to speak against the system in a strategic way. More like a call to action. Everything was intentionally designed to stimulate a revolution.

My mixtapes evolved from confessions to manifestos.

Tru and I put together multimedia art displays. There were images of victims: fathers, sons, daughters. It was like the faces had been frozen in time. Then, we showed footage of peaceful protests and pushes for change. I could tell that this was history in the making.

We also launched a series of shirts and posters. Tru was the visionary that linked the raw, gritty images of the streets to fashion.

The Ballot or the Bullet was the motto that inspired this movement. Bold, unapologetic t-shirts that made a powerful declaration to the system. I helped design the posters, but Tru worked the magic. The posters had the same sharpness, the same intensity, only now they were everywhere. Sticking out like a sore thumb on street corners, on bus stops, in the hands of people who weren't just tired, but ready.

"David, you're not just creating," she said while we hung new posters.

"This is an awakening. You've started a movement. I hope you're ready for it."

I smiled, then said, "I was born ready. Ain't no turning back now."

She smiled back. "Ok cool. Let's do it."

We were out on the streets the night before the protest, putting up posters, handing out flyers, making sure everyone knew the march was happening the next day. The energy of the city was hard to describe.

We never saw anything like this before, but this was *our* protest. The streets were filled with people wearing the t-shirts and holding posters.

I stood at the front with Tru, watching as people flooded the streets, moving in harmony, flowing together like a river that could no longer be stopped. The weight of what we'd created hung in the air like an unbroken promise.

"Do you hear them?" Tru asked.

I really did. It was amazing.

"Yeah. They're ready. This time, we gonna make 'em listen."

We marched with the mural behind us, the music in the air. This was about creating a force. A force demanding awareness. This was too powerful to *ever be ignored*.

The line between the booth and the ballot box was disappearing.

And Tru was there, every step of the way. Even though there was a lot of work to do, **together**, we were unstoppable.

Although the battle wasn't over, I knew who was with me. Together, we were painting a new future. A future where our voices could break the silence. And the world was about to feel it.

Track 12: Baby Boy, Grown Man

*"Saw my reflection in his eyes, now the muse is looking small,
Writing lullabies with wisdom, painting lessons on the wall.*

*Charcoal sketches of the past moving through the video frame,
A grown man's evolution, but the hunger's still the same."*

When Dave Jr. was born, I knew that my life started to change.

The storms of my past were passing through and a clear new day was here. My whole life consisted of me running from everything. Mostly, from becoming the man I was supposed to be. But holding my son against my chest, all excuses disappeared.

This small human being was dependent on me. No matter what.

As he looked into my eyes, I knew that I could never let him down. He was my responsibility.

Forever.

My son.

I could see my future in the depths of his eyes. And his eyes said to me that the world will shift through him. He would *see things I've never seen and feel things that I would never comprehend.*

DJ was more than another child.

He was the catalyst.

My legacy.

And anything I believed about manhood suddenly transformed.

"David," Tru stood next to me. Her eyes were soft as she looked at him.

"He's perfect."

I just shook my head. Attempting to hold back my emotions.

It was hard to find the best words in that moment. Almost like God knew that I needed to be silent. Nothing in my life ever felt this good. Every ounce of my pride had been exchanged with peace, clarity, and vulnerability.

I never knew that I was capable of this kind of love. He was my heart in human form.

Then, the days and nights were sleepless, busy, and long. I would be up at random hours changing diapers and rocking him back to sleep. Tru needed to rest, especially after having the baby. So, I wanted to be there for her and Dave Jr. every moment, every single day. She was always there for me through my best and lowest moments. Tru and DJ needed me, like I needed them. We are family.

This was a different phase of life for us both. Neither Tru nor I had a traditional family background. But when she looked at our son, there was always an awe like seeing him for the first time. I understood because she had never been a mother.

The way she held him, it was like he was the answer to unspoken prayers. I believe God heard the desire of our hearts.

It became clear that I found my muse. My reason to continue.

Now it seemed like I was being redirected. My entire focus for creating was changing. God gave me something to fight for. Something to protect, teach, and love more than anything else. There wasn't nothing wrong with hustlin', but it was no longer desperation. This was being obedient to my Creator.

So, I was inspired to write a simple children's book.

These were stories and lessons that I would pass on to DJ when he got older. Many of the stories were things that I was never taught, or heard growing up. Powerful teachings on love, hope, and faith, having the inner resolve to withstand challenges.

The writing and illustrations were both done by me. I used colors and textures that told their own story. Each page was a lesson. This was a story that he would learn from as an old man.

I knew that Tru didn't understand it. But she never questioned me. But if there was anyone that I wanted to understand, it was her.

"David," she said while on the couch, holding DJ as he slept, "This book isn't only for him, is it?"

For a second, I stopped because it confused me why she asked that. But then, I looked at all the pages, and knew that this was about me and Dave Jr.

"No. It's for me, too. This was how I could **rewrite my past by writing his future.**"

She leaned back and looked at me, then said with comfort.

"Keep writing, painting, and creating. If the world don't get it, that's their problem."

The book became a bigger project than I planned. This project evolved into an animated series. There were sketches that I drew in black and white charcoal. It was as if I was manifesting scenes from his future life.

Contour lines, multifaceted expressions. With each story there was an opportunity to teach something new. We were showing the world how to survive in a system that wasn't built for you. But doing it through love.

It was never about the money. This was my gift to my son.

An offering toward who I believed he would grow to be.

One night, I was in the studio just listening to multiple beats. And there was a song in my heart that I couldn't escape.

This was my first time writing a lullaby. It was crazy because I never wrote much about softer feelings towards anything. But Dave Jr. changed all of that.

When I spit those bars for the lullaby it came from a different place. It was full of positive energy, inspired by my deep love for him.

And *nothing could break that.*

It was the realest thing I ever wrote. I told him things that would stay with him as a grown man. Many things that I was never told. And it felt better than good. That was all that it needed.

The next day, Tru was in the kitchen, rocking DJ in his cradle. When I heard her humming to him, I decided to play the lullaby.

"Check this out," I said, while the song played.

She looked at me and smiled. And I knew there was a wisdom that she didn't expect to hear from me.

"David," she said, in a quiet and proud voice. "I love it."

"Thank you," I said, as my heart raced. "I just wanted to pour out my heart to him. No matter how hard life gets, find your reason for living. Tru, he's the reason I'm still here."

She hugged me tight. So tight that I could feel the tears running down my face.

I didn't have to say another word. She already knew.

When it was time for the music video, we used a few black and white scenes from my past. There were shots depicting shadows of empty streets surrounding me, and rap battles on street corners. The goal was to make it outta the trap the world had set for me and my people.

But the animation was where everything hit hardest.

Charcoal drawings of my son's face, his tiny hands reaching out as the images of my past flickered around him. He was the bright light in the middle of the dark chaos.

It was the visual representation of my life's thesis: that the future *must* **overcome the past.**

This was my gift to my son.

I wanted DJ to know that he could have a different story. He could start his own path.

Better than me.

The lullaby project went viral.

It was never about money, but something even more significant. It was about sending a message to the world that black men, fathers, and lives **matter**.

The world needed to feel our stories, experiences, and pain. And I believe my son's story could change the course of other lives. Then, he would someday understand that he was the reason for me pushing so hard.

And as I looked at him sleeping in Tru's arms, the future stretched out before me, full of possibilities I hadn't even dared to dream of before. The legacy I was leaving was no longer just mine.

It was his. And it was gonna be something beautiful.

"Do you feel him?" Tru whispered one night, her voice barely above a breath.

I nodded, my heart pounding. "Yeah," I said. "I feel him. Every day."

I felt him and the purpose he represented. It was the purpose to change what wanted to silence us.

The world began to realign. There was a *shift*.

But this time, it wasn't about me going through a storm. It was the peace and stillness after it. The calm.

It only came into being when you understood what you are here to do. Why you are here. Then, who you were doing it for.

My *entire existence* on this Earth finally made sense.

Looking at my family, nothing else was more important, this was my future. He was my reason, no more excuses. The legacy starts now. The work I do will outlive me and remain for my family.

My **son**.

My legacy.

My purpose.

SIDE D - ON THE BALLOT: Power & Redefinition

Rise to power, leadership, and legacy.

Track 13: Angels on the Hood

"Barbershop aesthetics on the path, flyers in the breeze,
Taking corner-boy ambition 2 council halls with ease.

Amplified murals on brick, got spirits comin' alive,
Music & art is the language 2 help my city thrive."

They called it crazy at first.

Crazy like hope usually is when it shows up where it ain't invited.

I was pushing my son in his stroller down the block one late afternoon. Tru walked beside me with that steady, quiet grace that felt like armor. The sun was low and heavy, like the atmosphere of the city. Someone built a shrine on the hood of an old Caprice.

Burning candles.

Teddy bears.

Half empty liquor bottles.

Balloons.

Letters with ink bleeding through each page.

Names.

Dates.

Futures deleted.

Angels on the hood.

DJ continued to sleep, and had no idea the love, hate relationship of this city. This was the same community where it could "love" you so hard, yet still lead to your destruction.

Now heartache and anguish became our décor. My neighborhood learned to lament out loud while silence censored us.

"This can't be all we leave them," I said, feeling the weight of it all. We were raising our children to be defeated before they even started.

Tru didn't say anything immediately. But, she looked at the memorial. Then at our Dave Jr. Then at me.

"David, do you feel that *pull*?" she asked.

"Yeah, I do. It's time. I must do something more."

I was scared, but knew in my heart that it was now or never.

Being hungry makes plenty of sense.

That's familiar and not difficult to justify.

But when you have an assignment? An assignment will keep you up at night. *And.* You can't run or hide either.

Later that night, after the baby went to sleep, I took out my old notebooks with lyrics and some policy ideas.

It was all of the things that I had been purposely avoiding. Old flyers from protests. Drawings of black men with crowns at barbershops.

So, I decided to tape them to the wall. This was gonna be my strategy to fight this system.

A mix of civil rights images and hip-hop album covers.

Verses written in the format of campaign slogans.

I moved with passion in my heart, and the rhythm of 808s in my brain. This led me to create budgets and redevelop what had been destroyed.

It was time to transfer **pain into policymaking**.

Music and art were my native language.

My classroom was the streets.

There was no curriculum, I had to create it.

This was gonna be the sound of "new politics"...

That's why I called it ***From Corner to Council*** because that's the truth everyone wanted to avoid. Now the same people that once hustled on the block would impact policy. Change had finally come to the city.

I filmed the documentary raw and uncut. No suit and tie. Just my hoodie and jeans.

There were different images of me around the old neighborhood and city. The old blocks where I hustled, the barbershop where I got my first haircut. Abandoned schools that were recently closed.

Housing was a secure foundation we needed.

Education was a bridge the community was afraid to cross.

Mental health was a wound disguised by jokes and hard liquor.

But I never tried to edit my past. I just enhanced it.

I told them who I was.

All of my mistakes. Who I hurt.

Who I lost.

And what I had survived.

Truth always hits hard, and it don't hide.

That's why I knew the streets would pay attention first. They respected it before the news and media outlets. And before the public thought I was "safe".

My art was moving faster than the campaign.

It was a creative revolution.

We turned deteriorated infrastructure into masterpieces. Mothers comforting the heart and soul of the block. Fathers being the armor protecting the community. And kids displaying the spirit and humanity we all needed.

This wasn't about me.

It was about claiming what we deserve, and that was peace.

Every mural asked the same question in bold, unforgiving letters:

WHO ARE YOU PROTECTING?

Then we decided to go digital. Putting **augmented reality posters,** with QR codes, up at bus stops and closed liquor stores. When you scanned the code it took you to the content of the policy over beats and rhymes. I managed to merge the block and politics. We were now in the conversation. The hood was on the ballot.

Old heads nodded slow.

Young kids listened hard.

The system started sweating.

"You know they watching you now," Tru said one night, the TV glowing blue against the walls, my name crawling across the screen under the word *controversial*.

I laughed, but it wasn't light. I bounced my son on my knee, feeling his weight, his trust.

"Good," I said. "That means they can't pretend we invisible no more."

Fatherhood had changed my aim.

The goal was about the power of safety and access. And I was gonna need power to have both.

Threats started coming in sideways. DMs. Anonymous letters.

I knew that I could only rely on my community for protection, not the state.

Life was changing. I began to love harder. And started prayer more than ever.

One evening, I brought DJ to see a community mural event. Cameras. Kids. Felt like the whole city came out to see it.

So, I lifted him up to get a view above the crowd. The art was super dope. Full of vibrant colors of black angels with locs and gold teeth. And their wings sewn together with faith, hope, and love.

"Can you see it?!" I said in a lower tone. "Now the city is dreaming out loud."

As I glanced at the wall, my son reached for the painted wings. It was like the angels were speaking to him. And he knew what was gonna happen.

Tears in her eyes, Tru spoke. "I'm so proud of you, David."

I looked at her. At DJ. Then at the streets that almost killed me.

"Yeah," I said. "For our son. For the future."

The city was filled with a bold confidence. Policy debates at barbershops. Voting drives at corner stores. The people that the system ignored wanted true *justice*.

Not only did the Angels come sit on hoods.

They also brought a sense of hope.

This was a new life that we were fighting for.

And this time we were gonna actually get it.

Track 14: Balance Your Energy

"Crossing lines 2 bridging gaps, with rhythm and flow,
Using portraits and the pulse so the people really know.

Basquiat style cover, Dirty South spirit in sound,
Governor Flow thru the speakers now we're reclaiming the ground."

There was an edgy vitality that existed in the air. When you came to the city, you knew people were fueled by the vibration of change.

You could feel it everywhere throughout the entire city. My name rang through every block and street corner. The music, art, and policy had connected our world. This was unlike anything anyone had ever seen.

Politics would never be the same. Tru, my homies, and the people of my city had a new radiant energy. This energy was gonna create a change that surpassed our imaginations. And I knew it was enough to transform the entire nation forever.

I was more than a candidate. At this point, I was becoming the medium for freedom. And with the pursuit of freedom there comes a storm. But we were ready, or at least we *thought* we were.

Art was the language of the people. We all became connected by the music, the visuals, the vitality of the streets.

And the new mural that I created was a collage of my life. It showed the rugged streets from younger days to polished floors of town hall meetings. Broken vinyl mixtape records to the beat of my public speeches. It was the souls of those who had been pushed to the side. But now it was time to be heard.

And Tru was there, her face in the middle of it all.

Meditating over it all, I whispered to myself, *"Energy".* The words spoke to me almost like a mantra.

There was a certain feeling that came when I said it. My music, art, and politics came from that place.

Life had become about the awareness and understating of that energy. This came from the pulse of the strong, tension of survivors, and souls of the voiceless. In order to succeed, I had to **balance that energy.** Become the mirror, both reflecting and guiding them, at the same time.

The people were following the movement because they saw themselves in me. Now that I had their ears, it was time to win their hearts.

And win their future.

"David," Tru's voice cut through the fog of my thoughts.

Her face was still flushed from the energy of the crowd she'd just left behind, fresh from the latest rally. Her hand brushed the back of my neck, warm and soothing.

"What are you thinking?" she asked, reading me like only she could.

"How to stay grounded, baby. How to keep this" pointing to the mural, the music, the vibe that we were cultivating.

"All of this from burning us out."

She raised an eyebrow, stepping closer.

"You've been balancing too much, David. Slow down, and don't forget one thing."

"What's that?"

"Balance. You gotta think about you."

She kissed me softly on the cheek, "Take time to rest. So you can recharge."

Not now, not when it felt like they were on the edge of something big. My campaign wasn't just a run for office. It was a revolution, an awakening, a revolution with a pulse.

But I could let the pressure cause the collapse of it all.

That's why I created the **People's Platform**, which was a traveling exhibit. This was my way of balancing all the forces coming at me. Finally, connecting all of the pieces together. It was an immersive experience that would establish true unity. And I wanted my campaign to be more than making empty promises that I couldn't keep.

It had to be a full experience.

The people needed to feel it in their bones.

So, my new album, *Governor Flow*, became the soundtrack for it.

Both music and art, on the album, established a soulful anthem in the new wave of politics. The raw energy of the graffiti made everyone look at the south in a different light. This visual declaration, clearing the path to the future.

The colors collided in a way that reflected the passion and promise in my soul. This was my way of showing the people the power that we already possess. I didn't want to hide nothing. Everyone needed to witness the authenticity of our neighborhoods, all the real shit going down in the trenches.

So I made sure that the beats and verses hit hard. The type of bars that made people uncomfortable, but also pushed me from the block to power. All of it was part of my story. Balancing the bad and ugly to produce something better.

But balance… that was a funny word. I was hustlin' hard, going nonstop. But I knew that I had to get it done. Honestly, I couldn't see it any other way.

"Let's take a walk," Tru said, pulling me out of my thoughts. *"You need some fresh air."*

At first, I pushed back but then I followed her outside. Instantly, I could feel the cold night air, balancing the intensity of my worries.

We walked in silence for a few moments. Then Tru started to speak.

"You gotta take care of yourself. Don't let this race break you, David. Don't let it break *us*."

I knew what she was saying. Winning was my primary focus, and *changing* the world, so much that I didn't give enough of me to the people who mattered most.

"You're right," I said softly. "But I can't let this go, Tru. This… this is bigger than me. It's bigger than us."

She smiled, a soft, understanding smile that always seemed to cut through his hardest moments. "I know. I see you, David. But you don't have to carry the weight alone."

The challenge wasn't going away, but I was beginning to understand how to handle it. How to *balance my energy*.

Because energy was everything. If I could master the chaos and the calm, then I would win. Not just the election, but the future.

The city felt different at night, everything appeared more exposed. It was like it was removing the old, to reveal the new. As I walked with Tru, the rhythm of her spirit was the only thing I could count on.

"Talk to me, David," she said, breaking the silence again.

"What's really going on in that head of yours?"

I wish I knew. But there were no words that could explain what I felt.

How could I make sense of a storm that was inside of me?

I didn't know how to say it. Not in words, anyway.

But Tru always understood, in ways I didn't even understand myself.

"I'm just tired, Tru. This shit is draining. I can't be everything to everybody."

As she reached for my hand, her fingers intertwined with mine.

"You're not losing yourself," she said softly.

"It's about maintaining your balance. The goal is to grow, so you're gonna be stretched on the journey."

She was showing me the value of conversing energy. I had to learn to be more balanced, the output and input had to support one another.

I let out a deep breath, staring out at the lights that flickered like fireflies against the dark sky. The weight of her words settled into me, but there was still so much more to process.

The streets needed me.

All the people were counting on me.

And deep down inside I wasn't totally sure if I believed them. Was it something actually unique about me?

Or was it the work?

Would the problems of my past get in the way?

"There's a voice inside of me saying, don't quit."

Tru squeezed my hand, and looked deep into my eyes.

"Yes, you can, if you need to. It's ok for you to rest. You've been fighting every single day of your life."

I was running on empty for so long and only knew one way to get things done. But maybe it was about pacing myself. I had to trust the process, even though I wasn't sure how to do that.

"I've been running, Tru."

"Running from everything. From who I really am, my past and my mistakes. So, now... now that I'm here, with all this happening, I'm afraid. Afraid that I'll be stuck in the nightmare of my past."

Tru's eyes softened, and she stepped closer to me, pressing her forehead against mine.

"Don't let your past get in the way of who you are becoming. You're not running away, David. You're running *toward* freedom.

A freedom that will change lives forever. And it's ok to be who you are in the process."

Her words were the calm that I needed in that moment. I was grateful that I had Tru.

And the people were with me. But my ultimate fear was possibly losing myself in the process.

"Maybe you're right," I said, after feeling the comfort of Tru's words.

"David, you can't continue to pour from an empty cup. After filling yours, then you can give."

We feel all around us that the city was alive. But in that moment, I knew everyone was trying to see my next move.

I knew that I needed to fall back. There was more power gained in not needing to control everything.

This was about giving myself the opportunity to grow.

The next morning, I woke up in a new way. Not full of energy, but at least it was manageable.

I had allowed myself a few hours of sleep, a rare gift these days. Almost as if God was telling me that I *didn't have to* **carry it all.**

As the sun was beginning to rise, it casted a bright light into the room. Tru was already up, standing at the window with a cup of coffee.

So, when she looked at me there was a quiet understanding between us. She didn't need to say anything.

My phone buzzed on the nightstand. I reached for it, checking the message that flashed across the screen. It was from my campaign manager:

"The People's Platform opens tomorrow. Are you ready?"

I looked at Tru and smiled more than ever before.

The **People's Platform** wasn't just an exhibit.

This was the result of years establishing music, art, and testimony. It was a true reflection of the streets and stories went untold.

No longer did I feel like swimming in a pool of problems. Now, I know that I carry the responsibility of the community and campaign. I started to believe in the promise of a new day.

I was running for office. But also, equipped to make change.

And change… was coming.

"Let's do this," I professed.

Tru looked at me, her eyes bursting with pride.

"We've got this."

Although the storm existed within me, I understand how to move forward.

When it's all said and done, I'm gonna be here.

Strong, wise, and ready to lead.

Track 15: Southern Man, National Stage

"Holograms in the town hall, murals blooming on the mall,
Turning policy to poetry so it's felt by all.

Projections on monuments, the Lincoln Memorial high,
One massive crowd-sourced painting reaching up 2 the sky."

It was becoming more and more interesting to me, how the nation started to view me. Most recently, I had become known as a force of nature. As if the trouble of my past had been a platform to transform me into a symbol of hope.

This was a journey that no one had ever seen before, including myself. The old ways of politics and government were long gone. I was everything that the public usually critiqued without shame. Now, a man from the deep south, raw and unfiltered, was making his presence known on the national stage.

There was no more political rhetoric, my campaign didn't need any of that to succeed. The people needed to be fully engaged in the experience, like a cashmere dream.

This was the transition into a new way of life. Transforming the spirit and growing within to fully understand who we are. Art and music were just the vessels to get there.

That meant, even our creative approach had to evolve. So, we put together holographic art shows.

My campaign team had worked with an emerging tech company to create this project. This innovative technology displayed huge, interactive holograms murals in city streets, parks, and government buildings. And each mural was an image of a real person telling their stories through abstract shapes, graffiti, and pieces of poetry.

This was art that demanded attention.

Each story was connected to my policy platform, to get my strategy to the public. I used art to address healthcare reform by showing the disparities. Visuals of lines to hospital waiting rooms, with messages about accessibility and affordability.

Music would pulse in the background, a deep, soulful bassline that echoed the beat of the people's hearts. The visualizations would change as the crowd moved, illustrating the systemic changes he promised to make.

When talking to my team, I wanted to understand the urgency of the moment.

"It's not time to talk about these issues anymore. We need to take action. But it has to be personal and very real."

Moving forward, each political rally and town hall was a cultural moment. When I came into a room, the lights would dim, then there would be an eruption of color. Live murals would be painted on the walls. And the crowd would feel the vibration of every brush stroke of paint.

Still, I knew deep in my heart the music would bring everything to life.

"Healthcare For All" was jazz-infused with spoken word verses explaining how universal healthcare could be put in place.

And I knew that *"Justice In Our Streets"* would become an anthem for police reform. Because I took the sound of sirens and mixed them into a soul sample, mixed with bars about justice and the fight for freedom.

The music policy translation, it was like legislation with a beat to it. I wanted it to hit people in their chest and disturb their spirits. My southern accent and deep voice would be the unnatural force initiating evolution.

Then, there was the big day when I spoke at the **Lincoln Memorial.**

You could see the history behind me, as I stood at the steps. The iconic pillars looming over me like guards, shielding the tomorrows of our country. Then, I saw leagues of people, beyond any distance that my mind could comprehend. So many thousands of people would want more than *politics as usual.*

The needed art. Culture. And truth.

As the night came, the crowd shouted with anticipation as I stepped onto the stage. You could feel the emotion, and I couldn't help but smile as soon as my first song played. And behind me, on the gigantic projection screen, there were images of people from different walks of life together, side-by-side. Peacefully.

The words of my platform flashed in massive, bold letters:

Equity. Justice. Unity. Freedom.

I paused. Then, as I started to speak I could feel the rhythm of the moment in my heart. It was like God put the words in my mouth because I didn't know what to say. So, I just poured out my heart and kept it real. It was time for a new system. And then, I did spit a few bars too.

This was a call to action, not a performance.

"Forget the politics. It's time for the people to stand together. Let's rewrite history together. All of us."

The crowd roared and so did the music. You could hear the 808s, bass deep enough to shake the spirit of the ground underneath. And when the last chorus blasted through the speakers, something happened.

The projections shifted again.

People of every race, nationality, and color started to come together. Black, White, Latino, Indigenous, Asian, and more. Everyone's eyes hopeful and proud, focused on the screen. And then, painting was finally complete. *Thousands of people* UNITED to create in real-time, a larger-than-life image, using their smartphones.

The painting was titled **The New Union**. And it was a reminder that no matter the mistakes of your past there's always something better on the way. As I put the final touches on the piece, you could hear the roars of the crowd for miles. This was more than any vision that I ever had. Everyone in the crowd chanted my name.

"David! David! David!"

Tears slowly came down my face as I stood there watching a new day unfold. A man from the southern streets in this country was at the steps of the Lincoln Memorial. We finally made it to the national stage. And I could feel the energy of the people in the air.

The power of art. The weight of what was possible.

My goal had become bigger than winning the election. This was the chance to rewrite history, and a new type of leadership.

The day had almost completely got away from me, but I knew I needed to be alone. Tru was out, almost like she knew that I needed a moment to wrap my head around the day. As I witnessed the lights of the monument, it all got super real. I wasn't dreaming.

This is more than a dream. This is really happening.

Growing up, I never thought that I could be part of real change in the world. It was then, I began to realize that change first starts inside of me. And no matter how high or low God allows me to go, I would always balance my energy.

Not alone, but with the people who supported me. Together, we would manifest our own destiny. Some new.

A **New Union.**

Track 16: Vibrate Higher

"Walking through the hall of mirrors, every canvas got a scar,
Visual autobiography of how we traveled so far.

One last track 4 the kids, let the world hear the sound,
Gotta vibrate higher, so I can lay my burdens down."

Although outside the Capitol there were waves of people erupting with emotion. Yet, inside the rotunda, there was a more tense, deliberate silence. Before swearing-in, I needed to have ten minutes alone before the world required my name in history.

It was all a dream. Everything was executed like a private exhibition.

The display included timestamps of multiple stations. First, there was one of my old notebooks that had my first lyrics in it. Then, there was a piece of brick, spray painted with a halo, from the first housing renovation project I completed.

As I stopped in front of an oversized mural canvas, it was a reproduction of the *"Angels on the Hood"* memorial. This was a reminder that I was bringing my whole city with me.

"You're looking at the receipts," I could hear Tru's voice as she flowed into the room. She was beyond beautiful, and her gown glistened like diamonds dripping water.

"I'm looking at the cost. Every one of these pieces are pain turned into sermons."

As I continued through the exhibit, there was the final display. It was a digital screen showing a video for the last track on *Governor Flow*.

As the music played, the deep bass, blasting through the speakers, you could feel the air in the rotunda vibrate. The footage was like a retro tv show: blurry, grainy heat of my first summer protests. Also, the process of the first bold and vibrant colorful neighborhood mural. Even a slow-motion scene with kids laughing and playing, on a newly revitalized playground.

This was not for advertisement. It was faith in action.

The music transitioned into a continuous instrumental, you could hear my pre-recording throughout the hall. It was a spoken word message that was broadcasted on every tv in America. This was for those angels still on the hoods, the kids.

"To all my creatives, making art, holding a brush or music, holding the pen...

To the girls who choose to dream and the boys using their imagination to create...

They tried to say that your vibration was too loud. And even too much.

Not that there was a glass ceiling, but a concrete one.

But we're on a different type of time. Check out the frequency.

You survived it all, and now there's another layer to the track.

And the result is the masterpiece you all are creating.

You are not just a miracle. You are the force. The motion.

I am just the voice, but you are the heart.

Vibrate higher. Not just to be heard... but so they can't tear you down."

Tru stepped beside me, her hand sliding into mine.

"You have made the theme music, David. Now let's make the motion picture."

We walked out onto the inaugural platform.

I smiled from hearing the roar of a thousand hopeful souls. The windy cold air hit my skin but was balanced by the energy of the crowd. And as I approached the podium, there were people singing my album word for word, and screaming my name. It was the most grateful humbling experience of my life.

My speech began with a message of smart goals and strategy, laced with justice and peace. Also, I explained the objectives of the *"Neighborhood Equity Act"*, as well as *"New Union"*. Then, informed the people that the soul of the country was now alive.

The applause was rumbling, erasing any prior insecurities or doubts that I had. At that moment, I knew that I was fully equipped to lead the nation.

Then, as I left the podium, there was a wave of energy that shifted me into a new dimension.

I was escorted to an armored limousine, heading toward the White House. Everyone was silent and Tru was by my side, holding my hand.

"Anya, do you mind reviewing the Hub feed?" I requested.

As she opened her laptop, there was a great sense of panic on her face.

"I'm not sure what happened, Mr. President!? But *Soul Vibes*...the security system has been hacked. Everything is gone. All of it."

Puzzled, though still composed. "Get me a secure line to the site."

Then, I pulled out my encrypted phone, which was supposed to be the most secure device in the world. Dialed the code for the Hub's director.

No answer? That was strange.

Suddenly, the limo was occupied by a razor-sharp frequency of digital static. I remembered a similar vibration from the car trap. Why can't I *escape this sound*?

There was an instant pause in the static. And a computer generated, distorted voice, spoke through the encrypted device:

"Now, your gallery is closed. This is where the real art begins."

Unexpectedly, the limo swayed back and forth. My driver mashed on the brakes, while we veered across Pennsylvania Avenue. I noticed that we were blocking incoming traffic. The Secret Service agents flooded the outside of the vehicle, screaming into their lapels.

Looking out of the window tint, I saw a shadow figure standing in the middle of a small crowd. Initially, I thought the crowd was cheering but they had organized a protest. Each person was wearing a logo jacket from my old record label.

The shadow man touched his ear. It appeared that he was getting instructions by way of a wireless communication device. Then, he pointed in my direction, almost piercing through the glass.

Then, out of nowhere, I saw Anya's laptop powered on by itself. But the screen didn't show the Hub. I saw a real-time recording of my home.

At the front door, there was a red blinking LED light on the doorbell camera.

While holding my phone, there was a sudden, intense vibration. A text message from a blocked number was on the screen:

[VIBRATE HIGHER. BUT WATCH THE DROP.]

The dashboard lights flashed on and off. Then the engine went out. It was then, while sitting in the darkness that I realized the "static" noise would not just go away.

The inauguration wasn't a victory lap. It was the start of a countdown.

Me……The President, I was trapped in the dark. And the world was still cheering.

So, I had two choices of how to handle the "Drop"?

The Counter-Signal: Bypass the car's system thru manipulating the sounds and frequencies.

The Physical Hustle: Order the Secret Service to sidestep protocol get my family to safety, by any means necessary.

So, I went with the Counter-Signal option. Mostly, because I knew that in the streets, the answer was never to scream for help. If you got jammed up, then you find the weakness, where no one is watching.

The darkness inside the armored limo was absolute, a heavy, velvet weight that smelled of ozone and trapped breath. Outside, the world was still a silent film of celebration, people waving flags at a car that had become a coffin.

"David, what is going on?" I could hear the terror in Tru's voice.

"Get low," the only thing that came to my mind.

The hijackers were using a Phase Cancellation attack. They had found the exact frequency of the encrypted network. Then, created a neutralizing signal, which would silence everything around me.

"Anya, give me your tablet. Now!"

"It's dead, David. The whole system is fried," she whispered, her hands shaking.

"It's not dead, but it is blocked."

So, I reached inside of my pocket, and grabbed an old mp3 player. MY thought was that it was old enough to not have a wireless chip. Then, I plugged it into the aux port, which I was surprised hadn't been removed.

I didn't look for a song. I was looking for a file I recorded in the basement of *Soul Vibes*: a raw, ultra-low frequency 808s sub-bass loop.

"What are you doing?" Tru asked.

"I'm changing the room's resonance". So, I cranked the volume up to the absolute max.

The limo didn't just play music; it shuddered. The sub-bass hit like a physical blow, a rhythmic thumping that rattled the reinforced glass and made the heavy steel frame groan. It was a vibration so high, so intense, that it began to interfere with the electronic components of the hijackers' localized jamming device.

Suddenly, the dashboard lights flickered to life, struggling against the static. The "Static" voice on the phone began to distort, its low whisper breaking into high-pitched, unintelligible chirps. I had created a "Drop" so heavy it forced the hijacker's system to recalibrate.

In that half-second window of electronic confusion, the limo's internal computer rebooted.

"Anya! Send the emergency bypass code to the Hub! Use the analog backup!"

Anya's fingers flew across the resurrected screen. "Signal sent! The Hub is back online! Security is locking down our house!"

Through the commotion of the booming bass, the flashing lights reflected on one specific face as they fled into the crowd. He was no *stranger*. It was a music producer from my block, who got locked up for hustlin' on the streets. This dude never liked me, but I never thought much of it.

The figure disappeared into a nearby metro, without a trace.

"Drive," I shouted to the Secret Service agent. "Get my son to the White House. *Now.*"

The driver mashed on the gas, tires screeching against the road. I fell back into my seat, with the rhythm of 808 loops still vibrating underneath me.

Tru squeezed my hand even tighter, and it was clear that she was ready to go to war.

I vibrated higher. I survived the drop.

When the White House gates opened, I understood the presidency wasn't a seat of power. This was a trap. And I was the only one who knew that bullets don't have names.

The first track ended. But the remix was gonna be a massacre.

HIDDEN TRACK - Epilogue: The 808s of Victory

The secret track.

**"Precincts bled blue, but Soul Vibes held the spirit of those left,
Finishing the contract for brothers we lost 2 the depth.**

**Crown made of thorns, and distorted frequency as the trap doors close,
Even though the ballot was won, still the war is just beginning to pose."**

Election night felt different than I expected. Almost measured, and cautious.

We went to Soul Vibes, for a sense of normalcy, and for a quiet place to just wait. The space was calm, filled with vibrant energy from the colorful murals. There was a very large screen over the empty stage, displaying a city map with colors as precincts reported.

Tru was next to me on an old leather couch near the soundboard, Dave Jr. slept on a blanket between us. As he dreamed, of course, he didn't comprehend the weight of the country on our shoulders. It was the rhythm of him sleeping, with the innocence of new life, that seemed to be the only thing I could trust that night.

But my campaign manager, Anya, was dope. She learned the political game from the streets. She was running, hustlin' numbers before she managed any spreadsheets. So, she was ready for the moment, it wasn't too big for her. That's why she was on the team.

"The margins are slim, David. They did everything to stop the movement. They attempted to vandalize the murals and questioned where the funding came from.

Even called the *Governor Flow* album 'inappropriate campaign material', but they can't stop the movement."

I felt every single word she said, but I didn't look at the screen. Only at my son and Tru.

"It never was about the numbers, Anya," my voice feeling sore from being on the campaign trail.

"It was about the energy. Did we move them? What did they *feel about the story*?"

"You did more than move them, David," Tru said softly, her eyes on our son.

"You *lit a fire inside* of them. Now, they have a beat in their hearts to march to."

The moment was one that I would never forget. The room was silent. Anya and Tru cried, along with members of my campaign team.

Then, I picked up my son, Dave Jr. And I thanked God for him being part of this special day. Yet, I understood that two things can be true: it was both the best and worst of times.

This wasn't winning an election. I was carrying out a contract.

The contract wasn't with the city council or the voters. It was a contract with the streets that raised me, the lost brothers who became angels on the hood, and my child in my arms whose path I had sworn to clear.

The victory wasn't the title; it was the access. The access to the table, finally, to be the one who could stop the neglect, to be the one who could fund the potential of the next generation instead of punishing their survival.

I stood in my new office downtown. The massive window showed a panorama of the city I now had the power to reshape. Below, I could see the corner where the mural of the winged child still stood, a defiant monument to the campaign.

Old D-Cash, the young hustler, would have thought getting into office was the greatest accomplishment. My Cashmere dream had been fulfilled. The escape complete.

But as *the visionary* in me knew this was just the beginning.

The beat goes on. The hustle continues, but only in a new phase. This was more than just art for survival.

Now the focus was establishing policy to improve the quality of others' lives. Those 808s on my mixtapes had become the instrumentals for laws and executive orders.

My first drafted legislation was to secure public funding for *Soul Vibes*—not as a Community Resilience and Creative Development Hub.

This former church now provided art and music education, mental health services, and job training. Like roads or utilities, this art space had been legally enacted as essential infrastructure.

Some criticize me as self-serving. But I thought of it as serving the community through a creative manifesto.

It was long overdue, but Tru and I got married. There was no doubt in my mind that she was the one for me. She was always putting in work, supporting everything that I have ever done. And at this point, it was just on a bigger scale. We were a long way from the old block of the neighborhood.

She ran the non-profit arm connected to the Hub, ensuring that the work stayed rooted, that the policy I made downtown never lost its echo from the corner.

The *real* battle began three months later with the introduction of the **"Neighborhood Equity Act."** It was a land trust initiative designed to buy up foreclosed properties in neglected districts, convert them to affordable housing and community-owned small businesses, and cap rent increases for ten years.

It was direct, aggressive economic warfare against corporate landlords and developers who took advantage of the community dry for decades. Those same private, special interest groups, and organizations, were the ones funding my opponents.

The backlash was *instant and venomous*.

The threats that had been whispered through DMs and anonymous letters now arrived laminated and signed by high-powered lawyers.

Town hall meetings devolved into screaming matches orchestrated by paid protestors. My every personal expense, every late-night studio session, every interaction with Tru was scrutinized, leaked, and weaponized.

"They're not fighting the policy, David," Anya warned one morning, slamming a newspaper onto my desk, the headline screaming about *Cashmere's Corruption*. "They're fighting the change agent. They want to scare you back into the studio, back into silence."

I refused to back down. We held a rally in the heart of the district the Act was designed to save. I stood on the makeshift stage, not in a suit, but in a clean hoodie and jeans, looking out at thousands of faces—my people, the *New Union*.

"They say this bill is radical!" I shouted into the mic, the bass of the accompanying beat vibrating the pavement.

"What's radical is ignoring our pain! What's radical is building luxury condos on the graves of our neighbors! We voted for change. Now we are DEMANDING justice!"

The crowd roared. The energy was pure, unfiltered *passion*.

That night, after the rally, I was driving home alone. Tru and Dave Jr. were already there, tucked in and waiting.

The city was quiet, dark, and damp. I took the longer route, passing Soul Vibes soaking up the quiet pride of the place.

I was three blocks away from home when the radio station playing my album, *Governor Flow*, suddenly cut out. The music was replaced by a sharp, deafening static.

I frowned, tapping the power button, but the static remained—a high-pitched, metallic shriek that felt like it was drilling directly into my skull.

Then, the static broke. And a voice, digitized and low, whispered through the speakers:

*"You should have **stuck to the music**, David."*

The air conditioning in the car suddenly seized up, a sickly sweet, chemical smell filling the cabin. Before I could even process the smell, the doors locked with a heavy *thud*. I punched the lock button, but nothing happened. I pounded on the windows, the glass holding firm.

The same digitized voice spoke again, closer this time, amplified within the trapped space of the vehicle:

"The hustle stops here. The ledger is being balanced."

Through the front windshield, I saw a flash of movement—a figure standing directly in the middle of the dark street, backlit by a distant streetlight. They were too far away to identify, but they were motionless, watching.

Anya's warning screamed in my head: *They want to scare you back into silence.*

This wasn't fear. This was pure, desperate rage. I reached under the seat for the emergency crowbar I kept there, and as my fingers wrapped around the cool metal, my eyes caught a detail on the dashboard: a small, red LED light, half-hidden near the climate control.

It wasn't standard. It was blinking. Fast.

The sweet, chemical smell intensified, making my vision swim.

I knew in the instant before everything went dark that I was trapped, poisoned, and cornered. My final coherent thought wasn't of the bill, or the campaign, or the Council. It was of the two heartbeats waiting for me at home.

I slammed the crowbar against the driver's side window with all my remaining strength. The glass spider-webbed but did not break. The static returned, louder than ever, drowning out the sound of the impact.

My eyelids grew heavy. The figure in the road took a step forward.

I knew the gas would take me in seconds.

*But I was a **father** now.*

I had survived the streets, I wouldn't die in a clean, locked vehicle.

Using the last reserves of oxygen and adrenaline, I swung the crowbar in a wide, desperate arc against the *side* window, not the front. The sound was a dull, heavy crunch.

The glass splintered, but the window remained largely intact. I dropped the crowbar, used both hands to smash out the spider-webbed pane and jammed my shoulder into the sharp, jagged opening. A searing pain shot through my arm, but the fresh, cold night air hit my lungs like a defibrillator.

I struggled to stand, while gasping for air and wiping my eyes. When I leaned against the car, I noticed that my arm was leaking blood. Then, I looked down the street, there was darkness but I didn't see anyone.

The shadow man was gone. But I could hear the distant *hiss and crackle* of static blasting from the radio. It felt like the sound of the enemy, laughing at me.

So, I grabbed my phone, fingers still full of blood and adrenaline. But I knew not to call the police.

I wasn't sure who I could trust.

Head on the swivel. My eyes scanned the street one last time.

Still smelling the gas. And the static seemed to get louder.

I was alive but unprotected. Bare.

Open to the elements.

I called the only person I trusted… Tru.

As the phone connected, there was a penetrating, noisy distorted line buzz. And not just in the car.

It was everywhere.

When I began to whisper in the phone, tasting blood and chemicals in my mouth. With my voice raw, I spoke.

"Tru. Don't open the door. Don't answer for anyone. I'm coming to you...they know."

The final beat dropped. I was running the last three blocks, and had lost large amounts of blood. But still awake and completely exposed.

Was this a true **victory**?

Or had my fight for survival *just begun*?

Acknowledgements

To God, for grace I didn't always recognize and mercy I will never be able to repay. To my family, for being my foundation—even when I had to learn how to stand on it. To my son, again—because fatherhood didn't just change my life; it changed my direction. To every lesson, every loss, every setback, and every moment that forced me to grow—thank you for shaping the man behind these words. To the culture—the music, the stories, the struggles, and the soul of the South—for giving me a language to tell this story in the only way it could be told. And to the readers—those who see themselves somewhere in these pages—thank you for carrying this journey forward.

Author Bio

Sam Braden IV is a Nashville-born storyteller, artist, and creative shaped by the rhythm of the South and the weight of lived experience. His work resides where faith, struggle, and self-discovery intersect—drawing on real life to explore what it means to survive, heal, and evolve.

A father, poet, and visionary, Sam channels his journey into art that speaks to both pain and purpose. Whether through words, design, or creative expression, his voice reflects the balance between ambition and reflection, grit and growth. He currently works in business development and teaches at the college level, building pathways while continuing to walk his own. Cashmere Dreams is his debut—an unfiltered expression of transformation, identity, and becoming.